MURDER AT THE MIDNIGHT BALL

A PRESCOTT HOUSE MYSTERY
BOOK 1

JESSICA BAKER

CELESTIAL PEN BOOKS

*For my parents and my friend Audrey
who have always supported and believed in me,
and everyone has joined me on this journey.*

DISCLAIMER

One of the mysteries in this book began in A Lady Thea Mystery
Short Story, A Christmas Puzzle.
While it is possible to read this story by itself, for the most
enjoyable reading experience, please read A Lady Thea Mystery
series books in order, before reading this one.

1

———

JAMES

EVERY UNMARRIED LADY AT THE BALL WANTED TO dance with an eligible bachelor. That in itself wasn't much of a surprise, but James Poyntz hated having the spotlight on him. As a reporter, he had learned to stand on the side and gather information. Chasing after Thea last year wasn't too different from that. But it wasn't every day that his cousin Emma was presented in Court, and his aunt and uncle made sure that her presentation ball was spectacular. No expense had been spared making it a night to remember. He spotted more than one lord that he knew and several ladies.

"You look like you're being tortured." He turned. Lady Theodora Prescott-Pryce smiled over at him.

When he approached her last fall, he never expected her to be so open to him actually being her brother. When his parents who had raised him... not his birth parents... died, he craved having a family again. Aunt Helen and Uncle Neville had always been good to him, but they had a child of their own and it wasn't the same. Meeting Colonel Stephen Bantry, his birth father, was strange, but it hadn't filled the void and desire for a family that existed inside him.

But Thea had been more than happy to welcome him into the family. To introduce him to their mother, his birth mother, something he had given up hope of ever happening after the late Earl of Astermore died unexpectedly. It always felt strangely like a sign when Thea's father died that he wasn't supposed to meet his birth family. It had been something like divine intervention that put him on the same train with Thea that day last August when they met.

He had met Thea's younger brother, the current Earl of Astermore, briefly in passing, but Lord Astermore didn't know they were related and he thought James was just a friend of his sister and her friend, the former Mrs. Livingston, Wilhelmina Allen.

"It doesn't matter. Emma's happy."

Emma delighted in being the center of attention, spinning around the ballroom with any number of potential suitors while the girls stood to the side of the ballroom glaring jealously. Her gown sparkled under the glow of the lights, shimmering like tiny jewels every time she shifted.

Thea laughed.

"Would you care to dance?" she asked, holding out her dance card in a clear indication that he couldn't say no. His lips tugged into a smile despite himself and he took the card from her.

"I see Inspector Thayne has taken not one, but two waltzes." He was sure he would hear people commenting on such a scandal. At least one dowager lady would notice and soon rumors would swirl about Thea and the inspector. He was surprised there hadn't been any already. Thea blushed deeply under the dim lights of the ballroom. "Are wedding bells on the horizon?"

She snorted quietly and he raised his brow at her in return.

"Not yet."

He frowned. "Thayne hasn't proposed yet?"

Thea shook her head. "But I suspect it won't be long." She smiled tightly. "Did you hear that Mother and Colonel Bantry have been courting?"

He let out a breath. He had *not* heard that news about his birth parents. Nearly twenty-eight years was a long time to wait to be with someone.

"I can't believe she didn't say anything to you."

His mouth felt suddenly dry and he desperately wished for a drink. Something strong.

"A few months, maybe? They can't decide on anything so they've kept it quiet. Not the place, nor the time, or anything else. I don't think I would have known if I hadn't happened to walk in." Thea huffed. "You should talk to them."

He bit his tongue. He spoke to his birth father twice a month, maybe, and his birth mother less than that. Not that they hadn't made the effort to try to get together more often... there were dinner invitations and offers to clubs and tea and family events... but James had spent so long on his own that they didn't feel like family. Instead, it felt like twenty-seven years too late.

Aunt Helen and Uncle Neville and Emma were his family. They had been there for him for his whole life. And Thea loved him unconditionally. There were no strings attached.

But the Dowager Countess Astermore, Vivien, had told him to call her... his birth mother... it felt like she wanted *something*. To assuage her guilt at having given him up, perhaps. And with the Colonel, it would start off well every time they met and descend into awkwardness by the time the natural conversation faded away. They weren't family. They were two strangers that he had tried to insert himself into their lives.

"I'd rather hear about you and Inspector Thayne."

It was the easiest way to divert the topic. Thea would blush and stammer when the inspector was brought up and generally, she would forget whatever she had been pestering him about before. It was a little disappointing to see her narrow her eyes and frown. He would hear about his parents' prospective wedding again, he supposed. He could deal with that, just so long as she didn't talk about it tonight.

"I don't see him here," he continued, trying to move past the topic he didn't want to dwell on any longer than he had to.

She shifted, the color on her cheeks still bright. "He was running late."

"Oh?"

He smirked at her and she glared.

"He rang." The song ended and the music changed to the next one. "I do believe it's your dance, Mr. Poyntz."

He motioned ahead. "After you."

She took his hand. "It's a beautiful party."

"My aunt's been planning it since Emma first started walking." She laughed and he continued. "I'm thrilled to see her so happy. Surprisingly stressed, but Aunt Helen said that's normal."

Thea laughed. "I tripped on the way out of my presentation. I didn't fall, but some people still mention it. Emma did wonderfully."

They swayed to the music and she relaxed a bit. James spotted Inspector Thayne nearly the minute he entered the room.

"So, how exactly did the inspector sign up for those waltzes when he's only just arrived?"

She glared at him. He liked seeing her infuriated. It was a much better look on her than the shy and delicate girl he encountered almost a year ago.

"He should dance with Emma," he continued on. "She wouldn't stop talking about him last year after the shooting party."

Thea smiled a bit dreamily. "He does make an impression."

He laughed. Somehow, his cousin had missed the fact that the Inspector only had eyes for Thea. Emma lit up as she saw Inspector Thayne, crossing the room only to hesitate when Wilhelmina stepped up beside the Inspector. They did make for quite a pair.

Wilhelmina looked rather lovely tonight in a surprisingly simple gown with little ornamentation. By changing her name, she had mostly avoided mourning for a husband who had betrayed her so thoroughly. So few connected the sophisticated lady detective with the former Mrs. Livingston that she had no problem starting over in society.

She had gone through all the proper channels and finally managed to open her own detective firm. Thanks to Inspector Thayne, Constable Cooke, and the others that they met last year, Wilhelmina hadn't had a problem getting established. From what he understood of her business, many of the clients were wealthy society women who needed a more discreet touch in handling their affairs than a man.

The song changed and Thea stepped back, though she didn't let go.

"Have fun with your next dance partner." He smiled knowingly.

"Won't you escort me over?"

She smirked, a playful quirk of her lips, and for a moment, he could see the family resemblance. James bowed his head. "Of course. After you, my lady."

Inspector Thayne glanced away from Wilhelmina as he saw them approaching. It was clear to anyone with eyes that Inspector Thayne and Thea were completely enamored with each other, but it was surprising that they hadn't acted on it. Or at least, if they had acted on it, it wasn't something James was aware of.

"Thayne." He inclined his head. "Good to see you again."

"You as well."

Thea took the inspector's hand and moved back towards the dance floor. James stepped closer to Wilhelmina. Not so close that it would be indecent, but close enough that they wouldn't be overheard.

"You look rather lovely tonight."

Wilhelmina smiled. She didn't blush the way Thea did. She didn't rile up as easily either.

"How has your week been?"

She let out a tortured sigh. "I feel as if I've found every widow in London's lost dog or cat or bird." She looked at him. "I want more exciting cases. I miss looking into murders and thefts and *interesting* cases."

"Maybe Inspector Thayne has something you would be able to work on."

She frowned, glaring out at the dance floor. "I doubt it. I think he's the reason I haven't heard anything more from the police."

James frowned. That didn't sound entirely out of character for the inspector, but he also had no reason to do so. Especially not when he had been the one to offer Wilhelmina his help in the first place.

"For Thea, of course," Wilhelmina continued. "She wants to keep me safe, no doubt."

That didn't sound like Thea. She never had a problem with others choosing their own path.

"If you'd like, I'll talk to my uncle and see if he would be willing to move your ad in the paper. Perhaps somewhere that it might get a bit more attention."

She smiled and nodded. "That would be nice. Thank you."

"And in the meantime, would you care to dance?"

She hesitated but took his hand. The music was the perfect speed for them to sway gently, not one of the quick dances that Emma loved so much. It was the perfect tempo that one could hold a conversation if they desired. The other couples spun slowly around them, beaded skirts clacking against each other.

The song ended and James led Wilhelmina off the floor.

James hadn't realized how late it had gotten until he heard the chimes on the grandfather clock ring midnight softly beneath the music. He still had work tomorrow, but it would be in bad taste to leave early, especially at his own cousin's party.

"Help! Somebody! Come quick!" Emma shouted from the doorway. The music stopped playing and Aunt Helen stepped forward. The room fell silent as all eyes looked to her.

"What's wrong?"

"Mr. Swinton. He's in the garden. We were taking a walk and he collapsed and he won't wake up."

Emma didn't seem to be breathing. Her voice was frantic and quick. It was only Wilhelmina's hand on James' arm that stopped him from crossing the room to her.

"I'll call the doctor," his uncle said, walking briskly into the hall.

Inspector Thayne came forward and spoke to Emma before following her out.

From his arm, Wilhelmina frowned. "Shall we?"

"Hmm?"

"Follow them? To the gardens?"

He nodded. "Yes."

2

JAMES

The gardens weren't actually a traditional garden. The terrace had been transformed into a relaxing refuge from the rest of the house. It wasn't very large, but his aunt had created a space that was truly a paradise. It was a small area between the main house and the carriage house. The flowers and hedges were well kept and it was one of James' favorite spots to eat breakfast.

Mr. Swinton was slumped forward over one of the benches, his arm slung across the back of it.

James looked to Inspector Thayne. The man had crouched over the lord and pressed his fingers to his neck. "There's no pulse."

"He's dead?" Emma's voice was high and pitchy as she stared wide-eyed and pale at the man on the bench. "But... but we were just talking! How could he die from talking?"

Inspector Thayne stood and gently guided her over to the chairs. Wilhelmina sat down with her. She ran a comforting hand down Emma's shoulder, speaking in soft tones.

Thea hovered in the background, staring down at the body. Something in her expression was odd. It was strange, considering she had seen murder victims before and had never reacted quite like this.

"You knew him?" James realized.

"We... we've met." She winced and glanced away. "He is—was friends with Cecil. Simon Swinton. They went to school together."

From everything that Thea had told him, her brother Cecil had some poor taste in friends. Most of them were spoiled lords.

"I'm sorry."

"Don't be. I never liked him. Mother forbid him from setting foot inside Prescott Place."

She closed her mouth, and it was clear that she was done talking about it.

"Oh my!"

They all turned in unison. A man with graying hair and glasses appeared in the doorway from the house. He carried a medical bag, not that it would do much good in this situation. It was far too late for Mr. Swinton.

His uncle appeared behind the man. "This is Doctor Cooper." The man wasn't the doctor who used to visit them when he or Emma were sick as children.

"Well, this young man certainly had an unfortunate night."

It was clearly an understatement.

IT DIDN'T TAKE LONG FOR THE POLICE TO ARRIVE. JAMES supposed that it being a society party meant that they felt the need to arrive sooner, rather than later. Inspector Thayne walked to them and they spoke in hushed tones for several minutes before they rejoined the rest of the group.

"Inspector Haddington," Thea greeted warmly, her eyes lighting up in recognition. "A pleasure to see you again. Though I wish the circumstances were better."

"Indeed, my lady." He bowed his head, before turning to the rest of the group. "Mrs. Allen."

Wilhelmina smiled at him. "Inspector."

"Shame that you had to be bothered like this on your night off, eh, Thayne." The inspector shot a look between Thea and Thayne that James wasn't sure he wanted to read too much into. He knew that Thea had developed some sort of feelings for Inspector Thayne, but would she not have said something if they were actually courting? It seemed like a perfect recipe for heartbreak.

"This is Mr. and Mrs. Poyntz and their daughter Emma," Thayne introduced them, "Emma was with Mr. Swinton at the time he collapsed."

Emma broke into a fresh round of tears.

"I'm sure this has been a very difficult evening," Inspector Haddington said. "Perhaps it might be for the best if the young lady was brought inside."

James looked to Thea. "Would you mind taking her inside?"

Thea shook her head. "Not at all."

"The servants' stairs are over there. Would you mind taking her through downstairs?"

She nodded, wrapping a comforting arm around his cousin as she guided Emma towards the stairs. That would help avoid a little gossip for now, at least. Emma was in a state and it would be better if the others at the party didn't see her looking like this.

"I'm staying," Wilhelmina insisted.

James nodded.

"This is really no place for a woman," the doctor protested, but she silenced him with a saccharine smile.

"I'm a private detective, Doctor Cooper. I'm afraid it'll take a bit more than this to frighten me." She reached into her purse and placed her card in the doctor's hands.

His uncle frowned. "A lady detective?"

Inspector Haddington flashed a grin at Uncle Neville. "There's actually been a number of female private detectives that have been employed by Scotland Yard." His face turned serious as he turned back to the doctor. "I don't mind if Mrs. Allen stays. Doesn't sound like there's much to be seen anyway."

"But—"

"Is there any reason to suspect foul play?"

The doctor opened his mouth to protest again, but seemed to realize it would be pointless. "No, but he was a young man who died quite suddenly. That alone seems suspicious."

"Noted. Thank you for your time tonight, Doctor."

The doctor bowed his head.

"I'll see you out, Doctor Cooper," Uncle Neville said as he came to the doctor's side. No doubt there would be quite a stir inside. Emma had to have been terribly frightened.

"Do you really think he died naturally?" he felt compelled to ask the inspectors.

Thayne let out a breath. "Because of who his family is and because of the sudden nature of his death, it's hard to say anything until the coroner examines him."

Inspector Haddington nodded in agreement.

"I'm sorry that it's caused such a stir this evening. I hope that your daughter is all right."

His uncle managed to keep a calm look upon his face. "Thank you for coming so quickly."

3

WILHELMINA

Wilhelmina walked into her office, if it could even be called that. The small, cramped space had once been part of the carriage house behind Prescott House. As they replaced their carriage with a car, they no longer were using that particular piece of space.

From the minor cases she had worked, renting an actual office wasn't worth the cost. It was fortunate that Thea's mother, the Countess —as all who lived in Prescott House called her— allowed her to use the space for free. What money she did earn could be saved up towards the day she could rent a proper space with her name on the door.

Beyond the abnormally low rent that she couldn't beat anywhere, the other advantage of using the carriage house at Prescott House as her office meant that it was already in a socially acceptable part of town. Not only that, it was discreet to come to. This meant her client, for one of the few real cases she had received so far of a young woman looking to prove her husband's adultery, had been able to meet her without arousing suspicion that she was meeting with an investigator.

The phone rang and Wilhelmina stared at it. Someday, she

would be able to afford the wages for a secretary. A secretary who would be able to answer the phone for her.

It was strange that someone like Thea was more comfortable using a telephone than Wilhelmina was. Perhaps it had something to do with her late husband refusing to put one in their house. Some nights Wilhelmina would walk in and hear Thea giggling on the phone in the hall. Since Thea didn't usually *giggle*, it was always clear that it had to be Inspector Thayne on the other end.

The phone rang again. Before she could think too much about it, her hand darted forward and grabbed the receiver.

"Allen Private Investigators. Wilhelmina Allen speaking."

She listened to the static from the other end. This was probably another prankster who thought it was funny to mock the lady detective. While she was far from the only female detective in England, she wondered if they all received such harassment upon opening their businesses.

"Wilhelmina?" he asked, as if she hadn't just said that exact thing. "Hello. It's James... James Poyntz."

She blinked.

"Are you there?"

"I'm here."

She heard him breathe and the crackle of static. "I'd like to hire you."

Wilhelmina frowned. She couldn't have heard that correctly.

"Do you mind if I come in this afternoon, say in an hour and I can explain in person?"

She shook her head before remembering that he wouldn't be able to see that movement. "Of course not. I'm looking forward to it."

She cringed as she hung up the phone. *'Looking forward to it?'* His cousin had been with a man when he died. It was likely James had called about that and she said that she was looking forward to it.

Her first client with an exciting case and she likely already messed it up.

Wilhelmina glanced around her office. Papers were stacked on the desk, since she didn't have a filing cabinet or a secretary to file them for her. The waiting room was non-existent. Her office needed a bit of work to be presentable for a client, even if that client was a friend.

AT THREE O'CLOCK ON THE DOT, WILHELMINA HEARD someone knocking at the door. She climbed down the stairs and opened it.

James Poyntz stood there awkwardly, shuffling his feet. Thea thought he was put together and confident. Having projected similar levels of confidence for years, Wilhelmina could see through that easily. His suit was crisp, his hair was brushed, but it was his eyes that gave him away.

"Hello."

She smiled. "Hello." She motioned behind her. "This way."

They climbed back up the stairs and into the office. It looked much cleaner and neater than it had before he called, and she was grateful to have had the warning to fix the office appropriately.

"Thank you for meeting with me."

"Of course." She gestured to her chair that was for clients and took a seat at the other side of the desk. He said he wanted to hire her so Wilhelmina was determined to appear as professional as possible. "Why don't you tell me what brings you in today?"

He took a breath.

"The police have determined that Mr. Swinton was murdered and the investigation appears to be directed at Emma. I don't have much information, but they've been to the house a number of times questioning her. The last time, they asked her to come down to the station to answer their questions."

That didn't sound good.

"I want to hire you to find out who actually did it."

Wilhelmina raised her brow. "You're sure Emma didn't do it?"

"I'm sure." He glanced at the wall behind her.

"Do we know how he actually died?"

James took a breath. "Poison. Please. I need to know what happened." He looked at her. "Whatever your rate is, I'll double it."

"My rate plus an article," she argued, and when he stared at her, she shrugged. "I need the publicity more. Most of my clients have been prospective divorcees and old ladies with missing pets. It's steady work, but it doesn't exactly pay well."

He nodded. "An article and ad space. For a proper advertisement, not whatever the paper would have given you."

That would be a blessing. The advertisement she paid for had turned out to be far smaller than most of the others on the page. Not only that, Wilhelmina was almost positive that the man at the newspaper made her pay for the larger space. Of course, no one had paid attention to it.

"Deal."

He grinned.

***

WILHELMINA STOOD OUTSIDE SCOTLAND YARD AS SHE waited for Detective Inspector Thomas Haddington to appear. Since he was the one who had responded to the call about Mr. Swinton, he would most likely be involved in the case and she wouldn't be surprised if he knew something about James' suspicions that the investigation was pointing towards Emma.

About five minutes after the hour, she caught sight of the inspector as he walked out with a group of other policemen. He was younger than most of the men that surrounded him by at least a decade, if not more, and like Inspector Thayne, it was incredibly impressive that he had made detective inspector at his age. He spotted her and she watched as he straightened up and said something to the other men. They nodded and he walked towards her, a smile across his handsome face.

"Mrs. Allen, what an unexpected pleasure."

Wilhelmina laughed. "If it's unexpected, then you're not half the detective I thought you were."

He rolled his eyes, but the smile didn't leave his lips.

"Is there something I can do for you?"

"Emma Poyntz." He stilled, the smile dropping away. "Is she truly being investigated as a suspect?"

He let out a sigh, running his fingers through his dark curls. "She was with Mr. Swinton when he died. I don't believe she did it, but there are others that believe being in the wrong place at the wrong time is a motive."

She bit her tongue. By that logic, Thea was incredibly guilty of three murders.

"Why do you ask?"

"Her cousin James hired me to find out what happened."

Thomas let out a breath, shaking his head. "I wish I could help, but I really can't say more. It's an open investigation."

"I understand." She smiled. "Perhaps we can take a walk sometime and you can not say some more?"

He laughed. "I'm sorry, Wilhelmina. I really can't bring you on this case. Especially not with you being hired by a possible suspect's family member."

"It was worth a try." She smiled at him.

4

WILHELMINA

IT WAS A BIT OF A CHALLENGE FIGURING OUT WHERE TO start. With the past murder cases she had worked, Thea had taken the lead and Wilhelmina had followed her to make sure she didn't get herself killed. James had always joined in to protect Thea. Wilhelmina couldn't exactly ask him for his help after he had just hired her to find out what really happened. Overall, she felt woefully inadequate for this job.

Perhaps taking up the case was a foolish idea.

"Mrs. Allen?"

She jerked upright.

Mrs. Poyntz hesitated in the doorway.

"Please, come in."

Mrs. Poyntz smiled, but it didn't match the proud grin she had given the other night at the ball.

Wilhelmina motioned to the chair and Mrs. Poyntz took a seat.

"My nephew, James, left your card in the hall. I hope you don't mind that I just dropped in."

"Not at all. I assume you're here because of your daughter."

Her brow furrowed and she shook her head. "I would like to hire you."

Wilhelmina motioned to the chairs. Mrs. Poyntz took a seat.

"How can I help you?"

She let out a breath. "Mr. Carter, our butler, said a number of pieces of silver went missing after the party. Then, while I was getting ready for dinner last night, I noticed that my grandmother's bracelet was missing."

Wilhelmina frowned. "You suspect someone at the party took them?"

"I'd hate to accuse anyone of such a thing, but it was so terribly chaotic the other night."

"I understand completely."

Chaos was the perfect cover for taking a few small trinkets. She doubted that the person who took these trinkets was involved with Mr. Swinton's death, but she had no doubt that they were quick to take full advantage of the opportunity.

"Have you told the police?"

Mrs. Poyntz laughed bitterly. "What's a few missing pieces of silver compared to the man poisoned at our party?" She shook her head. "They said it was probably an internal dispute."

"Have you hired any new servants?"

She shook her head. "Everyone has been in our household for years. None of them would do this."

She would be surprised, Wilhelmina thought.

It wouldn't be the first time that servants had stolen from their employers.

"It would still be best if I talked to them." She smiled, trying to put Mrs. Poyntz at ease. "They might have seen something."

Mrs. Poyntz nodded. "Of course."

"Would tomorrow work?"

She still had to finish up a divorce case. She needed to meet with the wife, Mrs. Rowley, to tell her what she had found out about her husband's affair. It would be good to wrap that case up and get paid before she set her attention on two new cases.

"Tomorrow would be fine. Perhaps you could join us for lunch and tell us more about being a lady detective."

"I'd be delighted to."

Mrs. Poyntz stood and Wilhelmina walked her out.

THE BENEFIT OF BEING A FEMALE DETECTIVE WITH A female client was that no one thought anything of it when she paid calls to her clients. It was often easier to go to them during their at-home hours so their husbands had no idea what was to come. Paying her call to Mrs. Rowley was no different.

She looked completely relaxed in her tea gown, sitting with a group of ladies that Wilhelmina recognized from various social events. She had never been formally introduced. Despite changing her name to her maiden name, her husband's reputation still hung over her in the social circles he was known in.

"Mrs. Allen," the housekeeper announced to the group.

"Oh! Mrs. Allen," one of the ladies greeted her. "You were at the Poyntz house for the ball the other night, weren't you?"

"Dreadful business," another lady dressed in green chipped in. "Can you imagine? Having the nerve to die in somebody else's house!"

"Honestly! Like he chose where he was going to die."

Mrs. Rowley was surprisingly pale. Wilhelmina hadn't gathered that she was particularly squeamish from their past interactions, especially when she told Wilhelmina that she thought for sure it would be easier to poison her husband rather than try to obtain a divorce.

She sat up suddenly. "I'm sorry to cut this short today but Mrs. Allen and I have a private matter to discuss."

The other women eyed them. It would be the subject of gossip for some while. Still, they filtered out and Wilhelmina took a seat.

"You found something?" Mrs. Rowley said, taking in the flat look on Wilhelmina's face.

Wilhelmina nodded and pulled the envelope out of her purse. "I'm sorry."

Mrs. Rowley had hired her to find evidence of her husband's affair. Wilhelmina expected to find him having a casual affair, not what she had found. Mr. Rowley had a long-term mistress. He bought many expensive things for her. Because one of the stores he bought from was Fletcher's, Wilhelmina even had bills and photographs as proof of them together.

Molly, one of Fletcher's owners, had been reluctant to give out customer information since it would be bad for business if anyone found out, but the bills had been helpful in proving the affair.

Mrs. Rowley let out a sigh. "I figured it was something like this. Robert—Mr. Rowley has been acting suspiciously for months now. I didn't want to believe it, but I'm not surprised."

Wilhelmina nodded.

Mrs. Rowley let out a bitter laugh. "I suppose this must be a rather common occurrence for you." She stood up, walked to a table and pulled out an envelope. "This should cover it."

Wilhelmina opened it briefly, just long enough to ensure that the money was actually in there. Counting it in front of a client felt terribly gauche, but she had been cheated by a few clients who thought it would be easy enough to take advantage of a female detective.

"Thank you for coming today."

Wilhelmina nodded. "Of course. Let me know if you need anything else."

PRESCOTT HOUSE HAD BECOME WILHELMINA'S HOME, ever since Ernest's arrest. Thea's mother, the Dowager Countess of Astermore, had been kind enough to extend the invitation and

Wilhelmina greatly appreciated the company. The Livingstons hadn't been the kindest to her in the aftermath.

The thought of her late husband made her cringe and she tried to push the thought from her mind.

Until Lord and Lady Astermore, Cecil and Ilene, arrived, Molly Talbot had lived with them. With the birth of her son, Daniel, named for his late father, Molly had moved in with her in-laws permanently, who wished to help her raise the child.

"Mrs. Allen," the current Lady Astermore, Thea's sister-in-law, greeted as she came down the stairs. "Off on another one of your detecting adventures?"

She smiled at Lady Astermore. "Of course."

"Dinner will be soon. I hope you'll join us."

Wilhelmina nodded. "I'll be down shortly."

She watched Lady Astermore make her way into the drawing-room before she headed upstairs to change for dinner. Thea's maid, Bridget, held one of her gowns.

"Oh!" The girl flushed. "I'm sorry, ma'am. Lady Thea told me—"

She waved the girl's explanation away. Thea was always sending Bridget to help her. Wilhelmina had no doubt that the maid reported back to Thea on what interesting cases Wilhelmina may have taken.

Since she returned from Astermore, Thea had been shaken by something. She spent an unusual amount of time hiding in her room, and Bridget had become her eyes and ears in the house. It only became worse when Lord and Lady Astermore arrived for the Season with their daughters, Lady Zoe and the newborn baby, Lady Louisa. Thea adored her nieces, but it was clear she'd rather avoid her brother and sister-in-law.

"Did she leave her room at all today?"

There had been days that Thea would only be seen at dinner, unless there was a social engagement she was required to attend.

Bridget grimaced. "She hasn't come back. She left right after

Lady Astermore and the Countess, and she didn't say where she was going and refused to let me come."

"Is she going to let me help with whatever it is she's doing?"

It frustrated Wilhelmina greatly. She wanted to help her friend, but so far, Thea had been unwilling to confide in anyone.

Bridget shook her head. "She hides something whenever I come into the room." She bit her lip. "I broke into her desk."

"What?"

"I know I shouldn't have, but I've been so worried. She's never not told me what she was doing."

Wilhelmina let out a breath. "And? What did you find?"

"Just some old newspapers. The society pages, mostly. There was a photograph of her aunt, Mrs. Seton, in one of them." Bridget shook her head. "It doesn't make sense why she's been hiding them."

It also didn't make sense why Thea would be focusing on her aunt again. Something had clearly happened at Astermore that triggered it, but what? Mrs. Dorothea Seton died six years ago, right before Thea's father passed.

"I'll talk to her about it."

Bridget's shoulders lost their tension.

"And she's probably just fine. She is probably with Mr. Poyntz or Inspector Thayne. I'm sure she'll be back soon."

Even as she said the words, Wilhelmina wasn't fully sure she believed them.

5

———

JAMES

"Why is this something we're looking for now?" James asked as they looked through the old copies of his uncle's paper.

Thea showed up at the newspaper office earlier that afternoon. Despite her insistence that she wasn't getting involved with any murders or mysteries, she had the same sort of look in her eyes as the last time.

"I can look tomorrow."

Thea clenched her jaw and he prepared himself for an argument. "I suppose."

"It would be a lot easier if you'd tell me what I'm looking for."

She glanced away.

"I want to help you, but I can't unless you tell me what I'm looking for."

He took a step closer and gently lifted her chin. To his surprise, her eyes had turned glassy and her lower lip trembled.

"What is it?"

"I think my aunt was murdered." He blinked. He knew better than to ask which aunt. "And I think my father might have been murdered too." She shook her head. "I feel so paranoid just saying it."

"What happened to make you think they were murdered?"

She swallowed. "My father—" She cut off, biting her lip. "It looked like he was investigating my aunt's death right before he died. I know after so many years, it's probably unlikely to find anything, but I thought—"

"I'll look for them tomorrow." James took her hand and squeezed it. "But you should be getting home for dinner."

He pulled his handkerchief out and offered it to her.

"Thank you." She wiped her face. "I feel so embarrassed."

He shook his head. "I'll see you home."

She nodded.

James had spent a fair amount of time avoiding most of Prescott House since the Season began. His relationship with his mother was awkward at best and he had somehow managed to avoid meeting Lord Astermore. It took him years to work up the courage to talk to Thea. From Thea's stories of their brother, he didn't think they would get along all that well and rather avoid it if he could.

Thea watched out the window of their cab. It had started raining on the way over, which seemed to fit Thea's mood perfectly.

It was always strange to him how quickly she accepted him. Anyone else in her position would have been skeptical. If someone walked up to him and claimed to be his sibling, he would have been skeptical. But she hadn't and he would be forever grateful.

The carriage came to a stop. James climbed out, offered her his hand, and opened his umbrella. The door opened as they darted up the stairs and Mr. Morgan, the butler, greeted them by taking James' umbrella.

"I need to get changed for dinner," Thea said as she pulled off her damp jacket. "Do you want to stay?"

He opened his mouth to say "no", because the last thing he wanted to do was eat in the same place as Lord and Lady Astermore, but it was hard to tell Thea "no".

"James!" their mother exclaimed as she came down the staircase. "I didn't realize you were joining us for dinner."

"I was just seeing Thea home." A quick glance out the window showed his cab had already left.

"Nonsense. Stay. I feel like I hardly see you anymore. Ezra can drive you home after."

He bowed his head. It was no use fighting her on it.

"Morgan, please find Mr. Poyntz something dry to wear."

"That's really not necessary," he began to protest, but Thea and their mother shut him up with matching glares.

JAMES ASSUMED THE SUIT THAT MR. MORGAN BROUGHT him was Lord Astermore's and it felt weird to wear another man's clothes while eating in his house. The shoulders were slightly wider and the sleeve was a bit long, but overall, it fit well.

He had been to dinner at Prescott House before and it was usually informal. It seemed that was something that changed with Lord and Lady Astermore's presence in the house.

Mr. Morgan helped him into a set of cufflinks that he was sure cost more than what he made in a year, and James couldn't help but wonder if Vivien had picked them out or if the staff was aware of his relationship to the family. Servants always knew more than what they let on, he found.

"Will there be anything else, sir?"

James shook his head. "Can I use the telephone briefly?"

"Of course, sir." The butler walked towards the door. "Right this way."

The telephone was in the main hall and James picked it up before asking the operator to connect him to his house.

"Poyntz residence. Mrs. Edwards speaking."

He left out a breath as the housekeeper answered.

"Mrs. Edwards, it's James. Will you tell my aunt I won't be home for dinner?" He barely waited for her acknowledgement before he thanked her and hung up.

"They're in the drawing room, sir," Mr. Morgan told him and James made his way there.

When he walked in the room, he would have thought he was seeing the ghost of Thea's father Matthew Prescott-Pryce, if the man across the room wasn't closer in height to Thea. He somehow managed to miss the man at any parties they both attended, and James had never seen him up close before. He never realized the striking resemblance between them. That had to be Lord Astermore.

Thea intercepted him by the door in a dress that rivaled the ones she wore to the balls, complete with gloves and a hairstyle that seemed complicated.

"Do they know who I am?" he asked in a low voice.

"No." She looked towards him. "I figured it should be your decision. Mother wasn't happy about that, but she understands."

He smiled. "Thank you."

He appreciated that she would allow him the space to make that choice. Meeting their mother brought up complicated emotions he hadn't realized he felt. Being in their home, being around them, he always felt frustrated that he hadn't had that.

James loved his parents, but they died from influenza when he was still very young, and his aunt and uncle became the ones who had raised him. He adored Emma and loved his aunt and uncle dearly, but he wished he had known his parents and his siblings growing up.

"I wish I had known we were having company. We're not even," he overheard Lady Astermore say to Vivien.

Wilhelmina smiled at him and Thea led him across the room. "So, you've been with her all day."

James shook her head. "Just this afternoon."

Wilhelmina sighed and shook her head.

James was surprised how long it took for Lord Astemore to make his way to them. If he had seen a strange man in his home talking to Emma, he would have come over much quicker. Though, from everything Thea had said, Lord Astermore didn't seem like the kind of man to be too protective.

"Mind if I join you?"

Wilhelmina's smile was tight. Thea's was non-existent.

"Cecil, this is James Poyntz." She paused. "James, this is Cecil… Lord Astermore."

"How do you do, Mr. Poyntz?" Lord Astermore greeted, and James could see why Thea had struggled so with trying to introduce him.

"How do you do," he said back. The awkward tension seemed almost palpable, and from the way Thea shifted and Wilhelmina looked down, he imagined that he wasn't the only one.

Lord Astermore seemed oblivious to it though, or he was much better at playing off the tension than the rest of them. "How did you meet?"

"My aunt knows Lady Ravenholm."

"We met on the train up to Ravenholm last year," Thea continued.

He nodded.

"I'm sorry to say that the ladies outnumber us tonight." Lord Astermore offered him a smile, but it looked forced. Very much a politician's smile.

"It's all right. I didn't expect to stay."

"Mr. Poyntz was just seeing me home. Mother insisted he stay for dinner," Thea told her brother.

Lord Astermore nodded.

It was fortunate that they were saved from anything more as

Mr. Morgan stepped into the room and announced that dinner was served.

'Saved' being a strong word.

"So, Mr. Poyntz, are you and Mrs. Allen seeing each other?" Lady Astermore asked after they sat down.

Wilhelmina's eyes went wide, and she shook her head. Lord and Lady Astermore seemed to miss her reaction though, and James wasn't sure how much they knew about Wilhelmina's work.

Wilhelmina swallowed and set her fork down. "Mr. Poyntz hired me to look into Mr. Swinton's death."

Lord Astermore hummed. "Horrible business."

If he hadn't known from Thea that Mr. Swinton and Lord Astermore had been friends, he never would have guessed from the lord's tone.

"I don't know how you can do what you do. It sounds so dangerous," Lady Astermore said.

"Not usually," Wilhelmina said, glancing at Thea. "It's usually safe.

Lady Astermore nodded. "I read your articles, Mr. Poyntz. None of that *sounded* very safe." She smiled, but James felt like he was getting ready to step into a trap. "Would you say that going after a murderer is very safe?"

He took a drink, swallowing his food before he spoke. "I didn't hire Mrs. Allen to find a murderer. Just to prove that my cousin wasn't involved in Mr. Swinton's death."

"Darling," Lord Astermore said, "I'm not sure this is really dinner conversation."

"If Thea and Mrs. Allen were bothered by it, they wouldn't be involved in such things."

From the pallor of Thea's face, she clearly was bothered by it. James had always gotten the impression that Thea had lied to their mother about her exact involvement in these cases. Not that he could blame her. His family didn't know half of what he was involved in.

James snuck a glance at Vivien. She had grown rather still, watching the rest of the table.

"I'm sure it's all quite safe," Lord Astermore soothed, but Lady Astermore didn't seem to believe him.

The rest of the meal passed relatively calmly, though there were a few pointed comments towards Thea's lack of a suitor and how brightly colored Wilhelmina's dress was for a woman who should have still been in mourning. By the time dinner finished and Lord Astermore led him into the library for drinks, James' muscles were tight from holding himself stiff.

No wonder why Thea found her sister-in-law to be a bit much to deal with.

"Forgive me if I sound too forward," Lord Astermore began as he handed James a glass of brandy. "What's your real relationship to my family?"

James glanced at him.

"My sister is rarely comfortable with anyone anymore and the only other people I've ever seen my mother so uncomfortable around are my grandmothers."

"Both of them?"

Lord Astermore chuckled dryly. "Indeed."

"Families are complicated."

"They are. And you didn't answer my question."

James froze. Why had it been so easy to tell Thea, but the words seemed to stick to his tongue when he tried to say them to Lord Astermore? Perhaps the distance between them didn't help. The man didn't exactly come across as the type to be happy to hear about his mother's pre-marital 'indiscretions', secret siblings, or anything else that might upset the balance.

"Ah."

James blinked.

"Sorry?"

"You're the child she gave up."

The words were said so matter-of-factly that James couldn't help but stare.

"You've known?"

"Suspected." Lord Astermore sighed. "Father had told me a little. Before."

"I didn't come for anything. That wasn't why I... meeting Thea was a matter of coincidence."

Lord Astermore stared at him, then snorted slightly. "Thea's both overly suspicious of everyone and overly trusting. She's quick to suspect the worst in people though. I doubt she would have ever invited you over if she thought you were using her... using our family."

"She thought I was a spy."

That brought a smile out on the earl's face. "Are you?"

James laughed. "No, but it would make a great story if I was." He shook his head. "I think there's enough intrigue in my life without adding espionage though."

"It seems so." Lord Astermore took a sip. "Thea hasn't gotten herself into anything dangerous again, has she?"

James shook his head. "It didn't seem like it."

Although, with so many years gone by, it was hard to say what might be revealed.

"She's been avoiding the house more than usual." Lord Astermore sighed. "Avoiding me."

"Were you both close?"

Lord Astermore shook his head. "It seems like the two of you might be closer. I suspect you know her better than I do, these days."

He wasn't sure what to say to that. Part of him wanted to comfort the earl. *His brother*, as strange as that was to think. But anything he said would have been false.

6

———

JAMES

J AMES HAD SPENT THE BETTER PART OF HIS LIFE AT THE West End Gazette. It had been his dream to write for the paper, and when his uncle finally allowed him to, he had been in awe.

That feeling hadn't lasted. It was hard work. His uncle had high standards for anything that would be in his paper, and nepotism only opened the door to a job at the paper. He still had to research every article to the same meticulous standards as any of his colleagues, and there was a different sort of feeling in that. Peace, almost.

He wanted to make his own name. His peers hadn't understood, but it was James who had to do the work, not them.

He was proud of where he was in his career. His uncle was less than thrilled about James taking an interest in war correspondence and had denied him that spot at the Gazette. Finding his birth father, Colonel Stephen Bantry, hadn't helped that interest dissipate any, but Stephen had been supportive and helped him apply to other papers in secret.

Finding out what happened to Thea's father and their aunt would be difficult, especially after so many years had passed. But the old records were a start, even if they hadn't found much yesterday. It certainly hadn't helped that Thea had been so reluctant to tell him what they were looking for.

Freddy Wright, James' old friend who often worked for the newspaper as a photographer, slapped a copy of the morning paper on James' desk. James glanced at the headline.

"Looks like the police still suspect foul play," Freddy said.

James let out a breath and opened the paper. "It's not something that's just going to go away. They have to explore all the angles."

Freddy glanced around, looking for anyone eavesdropping. "How's your family holding up?"

"Not well. Emma's... well, a man died in her arms. She's doing about as well as one can expect for those circumstances."

Freddy nodded sympathetically, but James was getting tired of accepting sympathies from everyone. He stared at the paper and hoped that Freddy would assume James hadn't seen and save him from giving the same awkward responses again. Halfway down the page, in the tiny font of an unimportant story, he spotted something that made him frown.

"Stolen?"

Freddy perked up. "What is it?"

"Who's Henry Phillips?"

Freddy laughed. "Shouldn't you know?"

James shot him a glare.

"He's downstairs. He's new. Trying to make a name for himself."

Weren't they all?

James folded the paper in his hands and stood. "Thank you."

After asking around, he was pointed to a desk in the center of the floor. Henry Phillips seemed too young for a desk so big. He seemed like a child dressed in his father's clothes as he sat hunched over the typewriter and pecked frantically at the keys.

"You wrote this?"

The boy lifted his head.

"Mr. Poyntz, sir. Yes, sir. Yes, I did."

"And the pictures?"

"I took them. I was supposed to be writing for the society pages, but then there were some items that went missing and—" He blinked. "Is there something wrong, Mr. Poyntz?"

James pointed at the photo. "This man in the picture was the one that died."

Phillips sputtered.

"Do you have anymore photos from any other parties?"

"Yes, sir. I mean, not here, sir, but I did take them. I can get them for you."

"That would be very helpful. Thank you."

The boy nodded. "Of course, sir."

James shook his head as he walked away. Had he ever been so eager to please?

SCOTLAND YARD WAS AN INTIMIDATING BUILDING. Perhaps it was just his nerves that made it feel that way. James eyed the building, before he walked inside.

Thea would be mad if she found out he had been here and asked, especially considering how secretive she had been about the whole thing. This was all a bit outside of the range of a mere set of newspaper clippings and it was time to treat it as such.

"Hello. Is Inspector Thayne in?" he asked at the front desk.

"Mr. Poyntz," Inspector Haddington said with a frown as he walked in the building. "You're not here about the death at your home, are you?"

He shook his head. "Actually, I was hoping to talk to Inspector Thayne about another matter."

The inspector frowned. "Police business?"

"I'm... I'm not entirely sure." The articles he had found were old and vague. His own memories surrounding the late Lord

Astermore's death were twisted at best with the resentment he felt at the time. To best help Thea, he needed to be objective.

"I can show you back there."

"That would be appreciated. Thank you."

"So, this possible police business, may I ask what it is?"

James hesitated. "It's for Lady Theodora. I promised I'd help look into something for her."

Inspector Haddington nodded. "Well, if there's anything I can do to help, let me know." He gave James a smile and knocked on a door. "Thayne, there's someone here to see you."

Inspector Thayne looked up from what he was reading, and Inspector Haddington nodded and walked away.

"Poyntz? Is something wrong?"

James stepped further inside the room.

"I was wondering if you'd be able to get me a couple of files."

He frowned. "For an article?"

James shook his head. "It's for Thea."

Thayne's frown deepened and he stood and closed the door.

"What did she get herself into now?"

"Nothing yet." He took a seat. "I'm hoping to keep it that way."

Thayne sat back down at his desk and watched him.

"What files?"

"The deaths of Thea's father and our aunt, Dorothea Seton." It was oddly easy to claim Dorothea as his aunt. Perhaps because he never knew her. "Thea has apparently come to the conclusion that they were murdered—"

Thayne pinched the bridge of his nose and muttered, "Of course she has," under his breath. James ignored him and continued on as if he had never been interrupted.

"—and she's been researching their deaths without telling anyone."

"Is that what she's been working on all these months?"

James shrugged and Thayne let out a long-tortured sigh.

"I'll see what I can do."

"Thank you." He turned to leave, his hand on the door when Thayne spoke again.

"Keep her safe, please?"

"I'll do my best."

"ARE YOU SURE YOU CAN TAKE TIME OFF FOR LUNCH?" Emma asked as they walked towards the Hargrave Hotel. The building reminded James of so many other grand buildings in London that screamed luxury and wealth. This was no different.

"I'm positive." He offered her a smile, but she was walking with her head down.

"I don't want to be a burden."

He reached for her hand and squeezed it. Anything more than that in public would be seen as excessive.

"You're not a burden."

The doorman opened the door for them and they stepped inside. The restaurant inside was one of his aunt's favorites and he hoped that the familiar atmosphere would be a comfort to his cousin.

Not even Lady Charlie's ball last night had brightened her spirits. He had been surprised to find Emma hiding in the library at Prescott Place rather than dancing with the eligible bachelors and gossiping with her friends.

"Table for two," he told the host.

"Of course, sir. Right this way."

The man led them through the restaurant to a table and left them to look at the menus.

"I know this has been hard on you, but hopefully, it'll all be over soon."

Emma's fingers tightened on the menu.

"How do the police even know it's murder? I don't understand who could do such a thing."

"You!"

A gloved hand thrust past his face, a finger waving in front of his vision.

"I beg your pardon."

The woman ignored him.

"You murdered my nephew, you little harpy."

Emma flinched back from the woman's accusing finger.

The Poyntz were upper middle class. Not quite nobility, though perhaps Emma could be if she married well. Times like this, it wasn't hard to remember how exactly the rest of society viewed the middle class.

"I'll thank you to step back," he hissed at the woman as he pushed his chair back and stood. "You're causing a scene."

The woman scoffed. "There should be a scene. This *young lady*"—the words were spat venomously—"should not be allowed out in public. She should be behind bars."

People were staring at them and whispering. James didn't mind as much, but Emma cowered behind him.

"Sir, miss," the host approached them, "I'm going to have to ask you to leave."

"Why should we have to leave? She was the one yelling," James said calmly.

The man looked nervously at the woman. "She's one of our best customers."

For a vague second, he imagined Thea showing up and their faces upon seeing her with them. It would be shocking for them to lose her business, as he knew that she truly was one of their best customers.

"James, please, let's just go," Emma whispered as she tugged on his jacket.

He nodded and they walked out. His fingers pressed into fists by his side, but he refused to lash out where she could see. He didn't want her to feel worse than she already did.

"I hate this," Emma sniffed as she wrapped her arms around herself. "I can't go anywhere without someone accusing me of killing him."

"I know somewhere we can go."

FLETCHER'S HAD THE SAME WELCOMING ATMOSPHERE IT had in the past. Every inch of the store invited you to step inside, come closer, and spare a second look. Unlike at the Hargrave, there were no accusing stares or whispers.

James supposed that having the amount of scandal that had surrounded the store in the past year probably did that. Mrs. Talbot and Mr. Fletcher had done an excellent job at hushing up those stories, but word still managed to get out. It always did.

The restaurant had changed very little in the past year, save for the grand piano that provided a soft undertone of music. More people were eating there and surprisingly, most of them seemed to be unchaperoned young women.

But even the beautiful atmosphere didn't seem to help lift Emma's spirits.

"I'm sorry to be wasting your time." Her voice was barely a whisper. "I'm afraid I don't have much of an appetite."

"You've hardly been eating. Scarcely sleeping." Emma started to speak, but he cut her off. "I heard you pacing last night."

"I'm sorry."

James shook his head. "Don't apologize. You need to take care of yourself. It's no good if you get yourself sick."

"I know."

"Do you?"

Her shoulders slumped slightly, her head ducking down.

"I know this whole ordeal is stressful, but Mrs. Allen is good at what she does. I'm certain she'll be able to prove you had nothing to do with this."

Emma let out a breath, though it might as well have been a sob. "It feels like a weight hanging over me. I keep waiting for it to all come crashing down."

He watched her.

"I liked him. I didn't hurt him. Why won't anyone believe me?" She sounded heartbroken by it, and he wished, more than anything, that he could shoulder her burden and take away her pain.

"I don't know. But we're going to find out the truth about what happened. I promise."

As the cab turned the corner, James couldn't help the sinking feeling that took over his stomach. He knew, somehow, before ever seeing the police on the doorstep waiting, that something wasn't right, and he had the strangest urge to order the driver to continue on.

When the cab pulled to a stop in front of their house, James spotted his aunt standing on the sidewalk. From her grim expression, he knew. They were there for Emma.

Inspector Haddington was amongst them. A frown was on his face, but from the other men with him, it wasn't by choice. James thought he recognized one of the men as a detective chief inspector.

"I'm sorry, Poyntz," Inspector Haddington said instead of greeting.

"Miss Poyntz," one of the other officers said. "You're under arrest."

7

WILHELMINA

WILHELMINA DRUMMED HER PEN AGAINST THE DESK AS she reviewed the case file on Mr. Swinton's death again. Inspector Haddington had slipped her the case file when she visited Scotland Yard, despite him publicly telling her he couldn't help her and couldn't talk about an open investigation. She wished the file had something more to go on, but the police did tend to focus rather single-mindedly on one suspect and ignore all of the evidence that pointed against it.

Even if she hadn't been hired by James, she would have known Emma couldn't have been the one to kill Mr. Swinton, just based on what she had observed that night. Natural causes seemed more likely than death by Emma's hand.

The case for Mrs. Poyntz's missing jewelry and silver seemed like a lost cause though. Despite interviewing the staff, there were so few leads. Too many people were in the house that night, but who knew if it had actually gone missing then.

Quiet was a commodity that was surprisingly hard to find in Prescott House the last few days. Thea's cousin, Lady Charlotte McNeil's grand ball had been held at Prescott House last night. Apparently, the house was grander than the McNeil's London residence, and Lady Astermore couldn't resist an opportunity to plan an event.

It amazed Wilhelmina that the woman could work in a snide remark in Thea's direction, no matter the occasion. Lady Astermore had managed to call Thea a spinster in the same breath that she talked about planning Lady Charlotte's future wedding.

What surprised her most was the fact that Thea took the comments without any protest. No one put an end to Lady Astermore's words.

Wilhelmina shook her head and looked back at the police report. It was so thin. The coroner's report hadn't been completed when Inspector Haddington gave it to her, and the coroner's office was no place for a woman who was not identifying her relative, unfortunately. She had been shooed from there more than once, much to her great dismay.

The door downstairs crashed and Wilhelmina jumped. A moment later, the door to her office opened, with Thea wide-eyed and panicked, a newspaper rolled up in her hands.

"What happened?"

"It's gone."

"What's gone?"

"My comb. It's gone." She paced furiously before the fireplace. "I thought that Mercury took it, since it was shiny, but I checked all of his usual hiding places and there were other things, but not that."

She was all worked up over a comb? Such a small thing... it wasn't like someone couldn't easily misplace one. Wilhelmina couldn't begin to count how many times she had set her combs someplace unusual after a night of dancing and not been able to find them the next day.

"It'll show up eventually, I'm sure."

But Thea shook her head and Wilhelmina recognized the look of Thea getting ready to be stubborn. Eventually wasn't going to be good enough.

Wilhelmina let out a breath. "When did you last see it?"

"Last night. I took it off before the ball. I was going to wear it, but I didn't. I left it on my vanity in its box and when I got back, it was gone. The whole box. I thought Bridget had taken it, but she hadn't seen it either."

"What's so special about this comb?"

"Les—a Christmas gift. It was a Christmas gift."

But Wilhelmina heard the first part of what Thea was going to say before she could stop herself. No wonder why Thea was so upset. A gift from Inspector Thayne.

"What did this comb look like?"

"It was a tortoise shell comb with diamonds. Shiny. Exactly what Mercury would play with."

Wilhelmina couldn't help but feel her eyebrows crawling higher. A jeweled comb was a serious gift. The implications of a male friend giving such a gift to an unmarried woman were more than Wilhelmina wanted to spend too much time examining at the moment.

It certainly explained why Thea had been acting as she had around Inspector Thayne the last several months. Months spent courting in relative secrecy. She wondered if the Countess knew that her daughter was serious about Inspector Thayne, though Wilhelmina imagined that the Countess probably would be supervising them much more closely if she did know.

Then again, the Countess had a secret son out of wedlock. Perhaps she was a bit more modern than one would think. And the world was changing. Thea could do far worse than a man like Inspector Thayne.

"I'll keep an eye out for it," she promised and watched as Thea's shoulders relaxed ever so slightly. "So, Inspector Thayne gave you a Christmas gift."

It was certainly amusing to watch Thea's cheeks flush brightly and her mouth open in protest.

"He's very handsome."

Thea ducked her head. "He is."

Wilhelmina smirked at her. It wasn't hard to see what Thea saw in the man. He was steady and dependable and exactly the kind of man she wished she had married, instead of Ernest.

The cases she took about a cheating spouse always drew her memories and emotions about her late husband to the surface. She hated it and wished she could bury it down where it would never again see the light of day, but Mrs. Rowley's case had brought those feelings back once more.

"I saw an article in the Gazette about things going missing. I just thought..."

She trailed off, but it was easy enough for Wilhelmina to fill in the rest. A missing comb was nothing strange. A missing diamond comb was a bit more suspicious. When similar things had happened at other houses, it was definitely something worth looking into.

"If you give me the guest list from last night, I'll look into it. I'm not sure I'll find anything."

Thea nodded. "Thank you."

For the second time that day, the door downstairs slammed open and was followed by frantic footsteps. James appeared a couple of moments later, hair wild like he had run the entire way to her office. His eyes were hard and he was breathing heavily.

"What happened?" Thea asked.

He looked at her, then at Wilhelmina. "It's Emma. She's been arrested."

8

———

WILHELMINA

"You know Emma didn't do it," Wilhelmina greeted Inspector Haddington.

The inspector let out an exasperated sigh as he set the files on his desk.

"I cannot discuss details of an open investigation with you, Mrs. Allen."

His eyes darted over to the other side of the room where she could see Detective Chief Inspector Morton glaring at her. If looks could kill, Wilhelmina would be six feet under already.

"Is there any possibility I can talk to her?"

Inspector Haddington shook his head. "Family and solicitor only."

She watched him, but nodded. "I understand."

How hard would it be to have the family say she was a relative? Although, she knew Chief Inspector Morton would never believe it. He had seen her there too many times and disliked her greatly. Having her sneak in wouldn't help Emma's case.

"Good day, Inspector."

"Wait by the Thames," he whispered under his breath as

Wilhelmina stepped back. She gave the slightest of nods to indicate she heard him and he straightened. "Good day, Mrs. Allen."

***

IF IT HADN'T BEEN A BEAUTIFUL DAY OUT, WILHELMINA might have given up on waiting for as long as it took Inspector Haddington to come outside. Her time would be better spent looking for the clues she needed to prove Emma's innocence.

"My apologies for the wait, Mrs. Allen," Inspector Haddington said as he approached. "I had trouble getting away."

She smiled at him, though it didn't feel as real as it could, considering the circumstances.

"I thought you should know, since you're working on her case." He glanced around, then moved in closer and dropped his voice. "The coroner's report was that Mr. Swinton died of cyanide poisoning."

Which certainly explained how they had found him and Emma's panic at the time. He would have had to ingest it only minutes before going outside with her.

"And when we searched the Poyntz house earlier, we found a bottle of mostly empty laurel water in Miss Poyntz's bedroom." He sighed.

Wilhelmina went still as Inspector Haddington continued.

"Taken in small doses, it's medicinal. A sedative. But it contains cyanide in the form of hydrocyanic acid."

Wilhelmina frowned.

"In large doses, it's fatal."

"Is there any way to test if the bottle you found in Emma's room is the same one that was used to poison Mr. Swinton?"

He shook his head.

A young lady's presentation and the countless parties and other engagements could be incredibly stressful, especially with the amount of pressure on her to successfully marry well and secure her future. It wouldn't be unreasonable for her to require a sleep aid to help her through such a difficult time.

"What was Emma's reason for killing him?" Wilhelmina asked.

And who else would have a reason to kill Mr. Swinton?

She tried to think back to that night. He hadn't been a very memorable person. It was almost like he blended into the background until he died, as horrible as that sounded.

THE GUEST LIST THAT THEA HAD PROVIDED HER WAS not much of a help. Between Mrs. Poyntz's list from the night of the murder and Thea's, over half of the names were the same. She knew Lady Charlotte and Emma were friends, so that made sense.

Wilhelmina needed to make progress on Mrs. Poyntz's stolen items, but Emma's case had taken priority. A murder was much more likely to make the headlines over a petty theft. She was just making assumptions that the person who had stolen from the Poyntz's house was the same person that stole Thea's comb.

Had anything else gone missing though from Prescott House? The newspaper Thea had left made it seem like others had also been victims of the same thief. Thieves? Wilhelmina glanced at the board where she had begun to pin up her cases. Who was to say that it wasn't more than one thief? After all, it had to be someone who had access to the houses.

Wilhelmina took a breath.

She had been treating these as separate cases, but what if they weren't...?

The telephone shrieked and she jumped. Heart hammering, she reached for the phone.

"Allen Private Investigators. Wil—"

"Mrs. Allen! It's Eliza Rowley. Can you come over?"

WILHELMINA STARED AT MRS. ROWLEY AS THE WOMAN watched the street below. Like the other times she was there, Wilhelmina noted the distinct lack of a male presence in the house. If she hadn't known Mrs. Rowley was married, she would have assumed she had been hired by an unmarried woman.

"The photos aren't enough proof, my solicitor told me." She turned back to Wilhelmina. "Can you find something more?"

"More?"

Mrs. Rowley nodded. "Would you be able to find the girl in the photos?"

She couldn't afford to turn down a case, not yet, but she wasn't sure how thin she could stretch herself. Still, she could probably find the girl in the photos with relative ease, especially since she kept her previous case files in case a client came back to her.

"Yes."

Mrs. Rowley let out a breath of relief and smiled at her. "I will, of course, pay you for your time."

"Of course," Wilhelmina agreed.

WILHELMINA LEFT THE ROWLEY'S HOUSE AND LET THE confidence she didn't feel fade away. How was she going to find the time to track down the girl in the photos?

It was one thing to say it, but she still needed to deliver on that promise or she would gain a bad reputation in this business, something she couldn't afford to do. There weren't many female detectives in this industry, not compared to the men.

It was time to go through all of her files again and start from the beginning. Perhaps the short detour to a different case would help her have a breakthrough on the other two.

"Long day?" She looked up at Thea as Thea walked into Wilhelmina's office.

"The longest."

Thea grimaced.

"What is it?"

"Ilene thought it might be a good idea to take Mr. and Mrs. Poyntz's mind off of Emma's arrest by hosting a dinner party tomorrow night. My aunt and uncle are coming, as are my cousins and James."

"Oh."

"Inspector Thayne too."

Wilhelmina's eyes grew wide.

"Why is she doing that?"

Thea sighed as she flopped into the chair in front of the desk. "I don't know. She wants to see me married this year."

Wilhelmina grimaced. Lady Astermore was insistent that Thea marry quickly, but at least it seemed for now that she had decided that Inspector Thayne was a good match for Thea. It was definitely a change from the beginning of the summer when she had made comments about him not being nobility. Which clearly was incorrect.

"If Mother hadn't told her to limit it to keep it small, it would have gotten really out of hand."

She could believe it.

Thea grinned wickedly. "I may have invited Colonel Bantry as well. I snuck his name onto Ilene's list and she never even noticed."

"Is this really the right time to be inviting the Poyntzs?" It seemed a bit insensitive with the timing.

"No." Thea sighed again and dropped her head into her hand. "And the fact that James' birth parents are going to be there is going to be..." She paused as she seemed to look for the right word to describe it. "...interesting?"

It sounded like a disaster waiting to happen. Colonel Stephen Bantry had been to Prescott House a number of times since Wilhelmina moved in, but never at the same time as James and certainly never at the same time as anyone else.

"Does his aunt and uncle know?" Thea grimaced and made a face that Wilhelmina interpreted as being unsure. "Does your sister-in-law know?"

"It's hard to tell. Cecil knows about Mother but I don't think he knows about Colonel Bantry."

She looked up. There was something deeply pensive in her expression. But she didn't say whatever it was she was thinking. Instead, Thea stood and walked to the case board. She studied it for a bit, frowning every so often until she spoke again.

"Rowley?"

Wilhelmina straightened.

"Not Eliza Rowley?"

"She's one of my clients."

Thea made a noise in her throat as her fingers traced the name. "I think she used to be friends with Mr. Swinton. I saw them together last summer."

Wilhelmina stared at her.

"It was strange that they always danced together one time at every party."

That in itself wasn't so strange. Plenty of people enjoyed each other's company.

"They haven't danced together this year," she realized as she stared at the newspaper clipping of Emma's ball. "Or have they?"

Thea shook her head. "I can't remember seeing them together."

"How very peculiar."

Something must have happened to cause them to avoid each other's company. Wilhelmina wished she had paid more attention last year, but her circumstances had been so different then.

She walked back to her desk and flipped through the photos she took of Mr. Rowley. Something in her gut told her that it was all connected. All she needed was a bit of luck and she'd figure out what exactly the connection was.

9

JAMES

"Poisoned?" James asked again as he sat in Wilhelmina's office. She looked remarkably calm for delivering such news.

"Poison is a woman's weapon," Wilhelmina pointed out. "It's not like it's completely outside the realm of possibilities for Emma to have done it. She would have had plenty of opportunity to slip the poison into his drink."

Emma... sweet, gentle Emma, who rescued wounded birds from the alleyway, poisoning a man? It seemed so utterly absurd he might have thought it to be a joke if the police hadn't arrested her.

James frowned. "That's all well and good, but you don't know Emma. I do. She doesn't have a vicious bone in her body."

"You're too close to her. You don't know what people are capable of doing when they're pushed to it. She could have done it, if she felt she had no other choice."

"But why?" James asked and watched as Wilhelmina frowned. "Why would she have no other choice?"

Mr. Swinton couldn't have been alone with Emma for more than a few minutes. Would that have really been enough time to poison him? To develop a motive for killing a man in cold blood?

Idyllic perception of his cousin aside, a crime of passion usually had a cause.

"Did they at least say how she did it?"

"Laurel water. They found a bottle in her room."

He nodded. "The doctor prescribed it. She hasn't been sleeping. The stress from all the parties."

Wilhelmina let out a sigh.

He supposed that she would know about the stress better than most, considering she had gone through it herself, and as a foreigner. His uncle and aunt had both impressed upon Emma more times than James could count about the necessity of her marrying well and securing her future.

"Is there a chance that the doctor will tell the police that?"

James shrugged. "I'll talk with my aunt and uncle. Perhaps he would." He sighed and ran his fingers through his hair. "It doesn't make any difference, does it? Just because it was prescribed doesn't mean she couldn't have used it to kill him, I suppose they would say."

Wilhelmina grimaced.

"I didn't think so."

———

THE HOUSE WAS QUIET WHEN JAMES RETURNED HOME that evening, and for that, he was grateful. He didn't think he could deal with much more at the moment. It felt like he had spent months in constant motion, always moving forward and thinking of the next plan. For so long, being a journalist was all he ever wanted, but in the last year, he started to find himself feeling more and more adrift. He hated that he couldn't stop wondering what his life could have been like if Vivien hadn't given him up, but he really had no time for dealing with "what ifs", especially with Emma's future and her life at stake.

As he crept inside, he could see a light at the end of the hall and his aunt and uncle's voices drifting softly out of the partially closed door. He didn't want to risk alerting them to his presence, because he wanted to know what they were talking about and knew that they would stop if they suspected someone to be listening.

"—going to court."

"What are we supposed to do?" his aunt asked softly. "Even if she is cleared—"

"When," his uncle interrupted. "When she is cleared of the charges."

His aunt sighed. "How will this affect her prospects?"

"Is this really the time to worry about *that*?"

His uncle's voice was far sharper than he heard his uncle ever speak to his aunt, but it was a tone James was fairly familiar with, and he couldn't stop his wince. His uncle was never cruel, not like many, but he did have a temper that came out in harsh tones, especially when it came to the safety of his family.

Emma's future marriage prospects seemed frivolous compared to that.

James let out a quiet sigh and edged back towards the stairs. He knew which stairs creaked by heart and kept close to the walls to avoid making any unnecessary noises that would alert them that someone had been listening the whole time.

In his bedroom, he pulled off his jacket and shoes and laid back on the bed. He was *tired*. One thing after another and he hated feeling so helpless. He wanted to do more. He wanted to be able to actually fix things and make a difference. He didn't want to have to stand by and watch as others solved his problems.

He couldn't investigate Emma's case. He was too close and the police would never take any evidence he brought forward seriously. But that didn't mean he couldn't do anything.

His dog, Muse, nudged her nose against his cheek and James sat up.

"Hi, Muse," he whispered as he rubbed her ears. "You know you're not supposed to be up on the bed."

She barked and climbed on top of him, and James laughed.

"You think you're one of Vivien's little lap dogs, don't you?"

Vivien's Blenheim Spaniels, Apollo and Artemis, were spoiled little dogs. They were always climbing on his lap when he visited Prescott House and always demanding attention.

Muse was a hunting dog though. He had gotten her several years ago and trained her from the time she was a puppy. She was the best dog he ever had, perhaps because she was only his, not a dog that had belonged to his family.

She barked, wagging her tail viciously. He laughed.

"Calm," he murmured, stroking her ears. "Calm down."

She grinned at him.

It had to be nice to be so carefree, to not know that anything was wrong with the world. He dropped his head against hers.

"Let's get a nice bone for you."

She barked again and James pushed her off of him.

"Let's go."

She jumped off the bed and followed him down the stairs towards the kitchen.

"James," his aunt exclaimed as she came up the stairs. "I didn't hear you come in."

He offered her a smile, though it felt plastered on his face. He wondered if she could tell. "I'm not staying long. I have plans for tonight."

It was a lie. He just didn't think he could face sitting down to dinner right now with his aunt and uncle knowing that he had failed Emma. He needed to be out there, doing something.

"With Muse?" His aunt looked down at the beagle skeptically.

He nodded. He hadn't intended to take her for a walk, but it was definitely better than sending her back upstairs or with one of the servants for a walk.

"I don't know when I'll be back."

He leaned forward and pressed a kiss to her cheek while she stared at him.

James didn't know where it was he intended to go after he left the house. Muse trotted faithfully beside him, staying close to his side. She knew better than to run when she was on the leash.

"I really didn't think this out," he told her.

She wagged her tail in reply.

He could have gone to Prescott House, but he hated to show up unexpectedly, especially with Lord and Lady Astermore there. Despite Lord Astermore realizing that they were related, James found himself even more reluctant to go to the main part of the house uninvited.

Instead, he let his feet wander. When he looked up, he found himself standing before Colonel Bantry's house. He had been there before, but it had been a while. His relationship with his birth father wasn't nearly as strained as it was with his birth mother, but Stephen said that he was always welcome in his home. As the Colonel's only heir, Stephen said that this was his home too. It never felt like it, but perhaps it was time for James to make a bit of an effort in the relationship as well.

James walked up the stairs and Muse followed him. The housekeeper, Mrs. Pearce, opened the door before he could even knock.

"Mr. Poyntz. Welcome. Will you be joining Colonel Bantry for dinner?"

He pulled his hat off and smiled at Mrs. Pearce. "If it's all right."

"Of course, sir. Please come in." She closed the door behind him. "May I take your coat?"

"Thank you."

He pulled it off and handed it to her along with his hat. Muse sat at his feet, calm other than her frantically wagging tail.

"Colonel Bantry is in the study."

He bowed his head and thanked her again before he headed

that way. His fingers drummed against his leg as he walked and Muse kept looking towards him, her head cocked curiously.

The doors to the study were open, though if the Colonel wasn't expecting guests, that was hardly a surprise. He was reading some papers when James knocked at the door, and Stephen looked up, blinking in surprise.

"James!" A smile spread over his face and James felt the guilt twisting in his stomach. He really should get better about visiting his birth parents if this was how they reacted to seeing him. "Come in. I hadn't expected you today."

He dipped his head. "I know. I should have checked—"

"Nonsense. You're always welcome here. I meant it when I said this is your home."

It still didn't feel like home. He loved his aunt and uncle and had lived with them for most of his life, but it didn't really feel like his home either. He had always waited for his aunt and uncle to get tired of him, which the feeling hadn't exactly lessened knowing he was adopted. If anything, it was worse. He would leave for most of the year for school and expect to not have anywhere to come home to in the summer. Realistically, he knew his aunt and uncle loved him and would never do that, but for a boy who had lost his parents and found out his birth parents hadn't wanted him, it didn't stop the fear.

Perhaps some day, he wouldn't feel that way, but James suspected it would be a long time before any place felt like home.

James let Muse off her leash. Stephen had expressed more than once that he should, and his birth father was fond of the beagle. She walked over to him and laid her head against his leg.

Stephen grinned and ran a hand over her silky head. "Hello there, sweet girl."

She let out a series of barks that sounded like she was trying to make conversation with him. She was a sweet dog, but she was also very vocal.

"Something seems to be on your mind," the Colonel observed as he set the papers down and motioned to the chairs.

James took the chair closer to the door and went to sit, when something silver and shiny caught his eye. Sure enough, a delicate silver card case had been wedged between the cushion and the back, enough that someone might not have noticed that they left it behind.

He picked it up and turned it over. He had seen it before, but the engraved initials on the front confirmed his suspicions. "This is Vivien's."

Stephen stepped closer. If James didn't know better, he would say the man looked almost bashful as he held out his hand.

"She's been coming to see me."

"Oh?" Not that he was owed an explanation.

"You're avoiding whatever brought you here."

"I am."

"Do you want to talk about it?"

James sighed and shook his head. Muse approached him and dropped her head on his knee, staring up at him with those big brown eyes.

"You'll hear about it soon enough, I'm sure." A scandal like this wasn't bound to stay quiet for long. "I just don't want to think about it anymore today."

"Then we won't talk about it."

Perhaps that was why he had come there. Anyone else would have pushed, would have forced him to talk when he wanted to forget for just a little bit. It was selfish of him to want that, especially when Emma couldn't, with her locked up and terrified. But he couldn't help her anymore tonight, and nothing he did right now would make a difference.

10

JAMES

Dinner at Prescott House wasn't nearly as awkward as the last time, though James couldn't help but notice Emma's absence. Lord and Lady Ravenholm had joined tonight, along with their son Lord Auldkirk and daughter Lady Charlotte, making the evening far more of a formal occasion than the small get-togethers that Thea was fond of hosting when her sister-in-law wasn't at Prescott House.

His aunt sat on the couch near Vivien and James wondered what exactly they were talking about. Perhaps commiserating over their children.

"James," Stephen greeted, and James swallowed.

"I didn't realize you would be here."

His birth father inclined his head. "It was kind of Lady Astermore to invite me."

Did Lady Astermore invite Stephen as Vivien's former lover or as Thea's favorite author? From his impressions of Lady Astermore, she was determined and stubborn and liked to prod at things that others would rather have left alone.

He was surprised to see Inspector Thayne entering the drawing room. Perhaps Lady Astermore paid more attention than he realized.

"I'm sorry to hear about your cousin. Terrible business."

James gritted his teeth, but nodded.

Across the room, Vivien walked in with Lord and Lady Ravenholm.

"James!" Lady Charlotte exclaimed as she saw him. She stopped mere inches before him, closer than socially acceptable. She kept her voice low as she spoke. "Is it true? About Emma?"

"I'm afraid so."

"How can they arrest her? It doesn't make any sense." She sent a sharp glare towards Inspector Thayne. For all the good that would do since the man wasn't assigned to Emma's case.

"I've been told poison's a woman's weapon. And that I'm not a good judge of her character."

She crossed her arms. "Anyone can use poison. The Lambeth Poisoner was a man and I'm sure there's many other men who haven't been caught."

He laughed despite himself. It was kind of her to try to make him feel not so miserable.

"I'm sure, but unless the police have another suspect handed to them, I doubt they're going to look."

"She didn't do it."

If he wasn't worried he would mess up his hair, his hands would have been running through it. It was a habit his aunt disapproved of and one he had tried to break since seeing Vivien do the same in his presence. Instead, he fisted his hands at his sides and wished he had a glass or something to hold so he had something to do with his hands.

"How do you know?"

"Because she had no motive." She stared at him as if she expected him to argue.

He didn't plan to, but Lady Charlotte was Emma's closest

friend. If there was anyone in the world that Emma would have confided in, it would have been her.

"Oh?"

She glanced at him, giving him a look that said she knew exactly what he was doing, but spoke anyway. "Mr. Swinton was handsome and the heir to his father's barony, but he was also rumored to be the heir to a distant cousin's estate."

She shifted, looking slightly uncomfortable and he knew what she didn't want to say. The Poyntz family may have money, but they had no titles to their name. Despite being wealthier than many of the aristocracy, there were those who would still look down upon them simply because they weren't titled. A baron's heir was actually better than most thought Emma deserved.

Not that lack of title and pedigree ever stopped anyone from marrying up in the world, he thought as he glanced across the room at Vivien and Lady Astermore. An American daughter of an Irish peasant and a solicitor's daughter. Both had married earls and had wound up with a higher status than the one they had been born with. Wilhelmina had as well, though he doubted she saw it that way after being cast out by her late husband's family and losing her inheritance in the process.

"Did you like him, as well?"

She frowned, but shook her head. "Everyone liked him. He was... charming. Made you feel like you were the only one in the room."

She sighed, but it didn't sound like the love-struck sound one expected a young lady to make over a handsome gentleman. Instead, it sounded weary.

"You knew him well then?"

"When we used to go to Astermore when I was younger, Cecil would bring him around. He was always charming. It was absolutely exhausting." She leaned in closer and dropped her voice lower. "Anthony despised him".

His lips twitched. He hadn't had the pleasure of meeting Mr. Swinton for more than a few moments, but if that was the case, it was understandable why someone would want to kill him. All he had to do was flirt with the wrong man's wife or make the wrong woman jealous.

"Your ball the other night seemed to be a great success," he said, changing to a happier subject. "I'm sorry I didn't get the chance to dance with you."

"You are?"

"Of course. It was your night. You've grown up so much."

It was true. She was no longer the awkward little girl he remembered hiding behind the walls of Ravenholm trying to catch a glimpse at the dance and spying on her brother. Even in the last year, she had grown more comfortable with herself and her interests, no longer hiding her passion for aeronautics the way she once had or letting other girls push her around.

But that seemed to be the wrong thing to say. He watched how Lady Charlotte seemed to shrink in on herself and wished he could take the words back.

"We could dance now," he offered as he saw Wilhelmina and Lord Auldkirk spin in the middle of the drawing room. It was nice to see Wilhelmina smiling brightly and laughing. She'd been so serious in the past year, and though she was still technically supposed to be in mourning for her husband, he doubted few would actually hold her to that.

Lady Charlotte shook her head. "I don't feel much like dancing right now." She licked her lips. "Oh, there's Thea—" and darted off.

Thayne approached him, offering a drink, and James took it gratefully.

"Not a word," James warned and downed the whole glass.

Thayne chuckled but kept blessedly silent. It was only luck that Auldkirk was too distracted to witness his blunders. He wasn't sure if Lady Charlotte's brother would laugh as well or challenge him to a duel. James wouldn't have been surprised to see Auldkirk resurrect the tradition just for him.

He had two conflicting images of Lady Charlotte in his mind. The girl he had met when they would go to Ravenholm and the young lady she had grown into.

Sometimes he forgot how to do all the things he pretended to be when he was interviewing someone or trying to make a good impression. It was a habit he had witnessed in Thea a fair few times, when she was comfortable enough that her mask fell away and she was no longer so aloof.

He took in her expression tonight, almost vacant with stony eyes. It was the same look that she had worn so often on the train when he met her.

"There's a story behind all that."

James glanced at Thayne, who stared at him with a raised brow. So much for not saying a word.

"Not a long one." It wasn't exactly the kind of story that would sell papers. Too straightforward. "My aunt was presented with Lady Ravenholm and they've been friends for a long time."

Auldkirk was only a year younger than him, so they had been thrown together when James was younger and his parents were still alive. As a child, he never thought it was strange that the Lord and Lady Astermore of the time never joined the Ravenholms. He hadn't made the connection about the late Lord Astermore and the current Lady Ravenholm being siblings, but in retrospect, it was strange. Especially seeing the way his aunt interacted with Vivien. There was more to the story.

When his parents told him he was adopted, not long before their deaths, he had asked them if they knew his birth parents. They said no, but he hated the nagging suspicion he felt that that had been a lie.

He closed his eyes for a moment and tried to remember when he was younger. He never saw Vivien at their house when his mother would receive guests. But he could remember seeing Lady

Ravenholm at his parents' house, and as he got older, at his aunt's house. She and Lord Ravenholm had come to dinner more than once. Lady Charlotte hadn't attended, being that she was still a child at the time, but Auldkirk had when he got older.

When he opened his eyes, Thayne was staring at him with a concerned look on his face, but James shook his head. He didn't want to talk about it right now and would have given a lot to stop the thoughts racing through his mind.

DINNER WAS STRANGE, MADE STRANGER YET BY THE fact that it was clear that only some of the people at the table knew the truth of Vivien and Stephen's relationship. Oddly enough, Lady Astermore seemed unusually oblivious to the tension for someone who had invited them all there. The ones who knew shooting glances in Vivien and Stephen's direction.

Though, perhaps even more interesting was watching the way that Thea and Thayne interacted. They weren't exactly subtle, but he hadn't realized how far their relationship had come in the last few months, not until he saw them actively trying to not act suspicious. There were no longing glances and no touches when they thought others weren't watching. He had watched them dance together through the Season, never more dances than socially appropriate, but Thayne's hand lingered just a bit longer than necessary and a bit lower than appropriate and Thea's body always shifted into him.

It was almost amusing that they thought no one else knew.

"I didn't know they were quite so serious," Wilhelmina muttered as she took a drink after dinner and watched them from across the room. "I should have realized with the number of times he's been over for dinner, but they haven't exactly been talking about it."

James took a drink but let her speak.

"He gave her a jeweled comb for Christmas."

He regretted the sip he took almost instantly, fighting to keep from choking. With sudden clarity, he could picture Thea and Thayne eloping and then continuing about their daily lives with no one the wiser. She probably was inspired by Mrs. Talbot and her husband's secret relationship, and look how well that worked out.

"They're not married," Wilhelmina laughed, like she could read his thoughts. "Do you really think that Thea would have put up with Lady Astermore's comments and attempts to match her with a completely unsuitable husband if she was?"

"Probably not."

"Not to mention, Lady Astermore has done this in front of Inspector Thayne more than once. I doubt it would go over so well if she was his wife."

James let out a breath. "You're right. I'm just a bit... the last few days have been hard and I let my imagination run."

The more he thought about it, the more ridiculous it seemed. But he had been busy trying to imagine the most unlikely scenarios in his head since Emma was arrested, so it wasn't so strange that he would see something where there was nothing.

He took another drink. "I just need this to be over."

He wouldn't think clearly until then.

11

WILHELMINA

WILHELMINA WATCHED MR. ROWLEY WALK INTO HIS club. She should be working on Emma's case, for James' sanity if nothing else, but all she could think about was poor Mrs. Rowley being forced to stay married to this man.

It wasn't fair that a man only needed to prove adultery in order to get a divorce, but a woman had to prove so much more. It had been one of the reasons why she hadn't looked for a divorce. It had been too impossible of a goal, but she hoped that things would change more in the future. And in the meantime, while she waited for that change, she could at least help the other women looking to do what she had been unable to.

Waiting for Mr. Rowley to emerge was slow and boring work, but it allowed her to read the reports that Inspector Haddington had struck from his office. The police had a bad tendency to stop at the easiest suspect, most likely because they were being pressed to close cases. But from her experiences in the past year, the first answer wasn't always the right one.

While she had expressed doubt to James, Wilhelmina really didn't believe that Emma would have killed Mr. Swinton. He was right that she had no reason to do so. But from what she had found out about Mr. Swinton, plenty of others might have had motive to kill him.

When Mr. Rowley finally emerged, Wilhelmina slumped. She was dressed in her plainest clothes, a part of her wardrobe that had significantly expanded since beginning this venture. Navy blues, grays, and browns, whatever helped her blend in best. And clearly it worked, since she never had been spotted.

"Where are you going?" she murmured to herself as she followed him down the street.

He seemed so completely unaware of anyone, but perhaps he had no reason to be paranoid. Perhaps he was going somewhere truly innocent. Something in her gut said otherwise.

He finally stopped at a fashionable building that was certainly not his house. A woman was waiting for him and she watched the two of them kiss. She recognized the woman as his mistress. She'd love a chance to speak with the woman and find something, anything, that would be incriminating enough to get Mrs. Rowley her divorce.

Wilhelmina lifted her camera and took a picture.

It was only a moment later she saw something flash out of the corner of her eye. The man lowered his camera, but it was too late. She had already seen him and set off after him.

Mr. Rowley forgotten, they raced through the streets. It was unladylike for a woman to run, but she couldn't let him develop the pictures. It would be a disaster for Mrs. Rowley if her husband knew she was having him followed.

Wilhelmina risked darting down an alley when the man went straight into a crowd. She knew the alley came around and she could cut him off, but there was also a chance she would lose him completely. The risk paid off though when she managed to come out in front of him.

Grabbing a cane from a protesting gentleman, she held it out and tripped the man off his feet.

"Thank you," she said as she handed the cane back. The

gentleman muttered some unflattering things under his breath that he thought she couldn't hear and walked off.

"Bloody bit," the man on the ground cursed in a thick, working-class accent, glaring at his shattered camera as he pushed himself to his hands and knees.

Wilhelmina kicked the camera out of his reach, and the man spewed another set of curses.

"Why were you following me?"

The man took a moment to collect himself and his accent came out different when he spoke this time. She noted it. Who was she to judge about trying to present yourself as something different than you were? Still, it was a useful thing to note for the future. "Why do you care?"

She cocked her brow and kicked his knee out from under him and he collapsed back onto the ground.

"I was hired!"

"By who?"

"Ain't gonna tell you."

They'd see about that. She pressed her boot heel into his shin and he cursed again loudly.

"Rowley! Rowley hired me." She pressed harder. "Bloody hell, woman!"

"Which Rowley?"

"Ro-Robert!"

She let her heel up.

"Can I get up?"

Wilhelmina stepped back and smiled down at him. "I don't know. Can you?"

The man glared and pushed himself to his feet, stooping down to scoop up the camera. "I saved for a month for this."

The accent was gone again. He was clearly trying to hide how upset he was.

He wouldn't make her feel guilty about it. She had been living with enough guilt to last a person a lifetime. Some stranger stalking her wouldn't manage to make her feel guilty again.

"And why is Mr. Rowley having me followed?"

The man clenched his jaw.

"I'll pay you for the information, if that eases your conscience any."

He looked like he was considering it, which was more than she hoped for.

"Fine. But let's go somewhere else to talk. My offices are—"

"No." She wouldn't go somewhere she hadn't been before. She didn't know him. Who knew what he would be willing to do to her? "I know somewhere closer. Mr.—"

"Shaw. Gabriel Shaw."

12

WILHELMINA

MR. SHAW TUGGED AT HIS CUFFS, THE MOVEMENT betraying his discomfort at the opulence around them. The cafe at Fletcher's was public and Wilhelmina knew the area enough to escape if needed. She'd never take a man she didn't know somewhere private and hope that she would turn out all right. That would be stupid.

"So you're a private investigator, Mr. Shaw?" she asked as she sat across the table from him, a pot of tea and some refreshments between them. His business card was printed on cheap paper and she wondered if his business was any better than hers. Being a man should surely give him a leg up over her. Perhaps it wasn't as much of an advantage as she thought it was.

"I am. Six years now."

She eyed him.

"And Mr. Rowley hired you to follow me... why?"

Mr. Shaw swallowed hard and glared at his tea like he expected it to be stronger.

"He knew his wife had someone following him. Wanted to find out who."

"She's trying to get a divorce from him, you know."

The man frowned. "Rowley doesn't want a divorce from her."

Mr. Rowley had a mistress but didn't want a divorce? There had to be more to that story.

"Wife's father holds the purse strings. 'e'll lose the allowance if she divorces him."

"Ah."

That would do it.

"His wife's been seeing someone too. He knew it was a matter of time before…"

Wilhelmina wanted to curse herself. She should have known that Mrs. Rowley was seeing someone else. It made sense, but she always was quicker to give the woman the benefit of the doubt that she wasn't the guilty party. Perhaps that should change.

"Before she tried for a divorce and wanted to marry her lover?" she finished his thought and Mr. Shaw nodded.

Wilhelmina closed her eyes and let out a breath.

"Do you have any pictures of Mrs. Rowley's lover?"

Perhaps he might be useful to track down.

Mr. Shaw nodded. "Back at my office. Want me to bring them over to yours?"

"That would be helpful. Thank you."

She pulled a shilling and her business card and placed them both on the table, along with enough to cover the bill.

"Good day."

"Good day," he echoed, before he took another sip of tea.

WITH SOMETHING THAT FELT LIKE PROGRESS MADE, Wilhelmina returned to the building where she saw Mr. Rowley and his mistress. It felt like luck that she arrived in time to see Mr. Rowley leaving without the woman. Perhaps everything wasn't against her today.

She waited until Mr. Rowley disappeared around the corner

and until she was sure he wasn't coming back before she crossed the street.

Which flat was the woman he was with?

"Ma'am?" a young woman asked as she came down the stairs. "Can I help you find someone? You seem a bit lost."

Wilhelmina nodded. "The man that just left—"

The young woman nodded. "Mr. Morris."

"I'm supposed to meet his—"

"His wife," the woman finished for her, nodding.

"Yes, exactly. But Mrs. Morris forgot to tell me which flat she was in."

The woman nodded sympathetically. "She's just upstairs. Second floor. Flat B."

Wilhelmina smiled. "Thank you."

What kind of woman was upstairs? It seemed like Mr. Rowley might have married a second time, which was exactly the kind of thing she needed to bring to Mrs. Rowley. But who had he married first?

She knocked on the door and was surprised by the age of the woman who answered the door. From a distance, she always thought the woman was older, but she couldn't be much older than Lady Charlie.

"Can I help you?" the woman asked with no small amount of confusion in her eyes.

"Mrs. Morris?"

She nodded.

"My name is Wilhelmina Allen. May I come in?"

The woman's brow furrowed, but she opened the door a bit further and allowed Wilhelmina inside.

The flat had everything that Wilhelmina expected to find in the Rowleys' townhouse. There were traces of a man's existence here, from the coat rack to the portraits. Wilhelmina could see Mr. Rowley in nearly every picture displayed.

"I'm afraid I don't know who you are," Mrs. Morris said as Wilhelmina looked around the entrance hall.

"I'm a private investigator." She watched as Mrs. Morris' brow furrowed. "I was hired to follow your husband."

"What? Why?"

How did one even break this kind of news to someone?

"Mrs. Morris, how long have you and your husband been married?"

The young woman's brow furrowed. "Last August."

Wilhelmina let out a breath, even as Mrs. Morris lifted a frame and showed it to her. Sure enough, there they were, both dressed in wedding clothes.

"Who hired you to follow my husband?"

"His wife."

Mrs. Morris stilled.

"I'm his wife."

"But not his first wife."

"But she died?"

Wilhelmina blinked. "He told you that?"

Mrs. Morris nodded.

It wasn't hard to picture Ernest doing something like that. There were times when Wilhelmina had wondered if Jennie, Ernest's first wife, had faked her death instead and ran away.

Wilhelmina sighed.

"Where does he tell you he goes when he's away for a long time?"

"His mother is sick. She—" Mrs. Morris cut off, a look of horror overtaking her face. "He's with her when he says that, isn't he? And when he goes on business trips and..." She sank onto one of the couches. "I feel so stupid."

She imagined that Mrs. Rowley was paying for the flat that Mrs. Morris lived in. Did this poor woman own anything that hadn't been bought for her by Mr. Rowley?

Wilhelmina set a hand on the young woman's shoulders.

"He said he's going away for business when he was just here. I should have known…" She shook her head. "He told me he wasn't having an affair with someone else, when I asked him. I thought for sure." The young woman let out a bitter laugh. "I guess *I was* the affair."

"I'm truly sorry."

"Another wife?" Mrs. Rowley asked. Her eyes were wide and she was grasping at her side. "I never would have thought… not in a million years."

Mrs. Rowley paced the room.

"Will she, this Mrs. Morris, testify against him?"

"She will. And I found the documents that prove they were legally married, along with proof that your husband has also been living under the name Mr. Robert Morris."

She flinched. "How long?"

"About a year."

Mrs. Rowley took a deep breath before she turned in one fluid motion, picked a vase off a table and flung it as hard as she could. It shattered against the wall, raining shards of porcelain down to the floor.

Wilhelmina jerked back. Such a thing shouldn't affect her anymore, but the suddenness of it and the loud sound scared her.

"I'm sorry," Mrs. Rowley said as she dropped her hand down. "I just… I didn't think."

She slumped into one of the chairs.

"I knew he was being unfaithful, but this… this, I could have never imagined."

Wilhelmina hated feeling so helpless. Giving bad news to two people in one day was a bit more than she usually dealt with.

"Where is Mrs. Morris?"

"She's safe. I relocated her."

She didn't want to risk Mr. Rowley doing something to try to make Mrs. Morris disappear before she could testify against him. It wouldn't be the first time a husband had tried to do something to get out of a divorce.

Mrs. Rowley nodded. "Thank you for letting me know. I hope this is enough."

"Are you sure it's alright if I stay here?" Mrs. Morris asked as she looked around the little bedroom.

Wilhelmina's office wasn't exactly the most luxurious accommodations, but it did have a bedroom and plumbing, since it had served as the coachman's rooms when the Prescott-Pryces had a coachman, long before Wilhelmina came to Prescott House. Since Ezra took the role of chauffeur and preferred to live in the main part of the house with his brother, the carriage house had been left empty. Still, the bed frames remained from when this had been the coachman's house and it would be livable until she could find Mrs. Morris more permanent accommodations.

Wilhelmina nodded. "It might be best if you don't go outside though. There's a terrace downstairs where you'll be able to get some fresh air, but it's really better if no one knows where you are."

She couldn't explain it, but she had a bad feeling that if Mrs. Morris went out and Mr. Rowley found her, she would never be heard from again.

The whole plan was almost ingenious. Mr. Rowley and Mr. Morris led such different lives, by both of his wives' accounts. They would never have a reason to cross paths. A baron's daughter and an aspiring actress.

"I'll stay inside then."

She cast a glance out the window.

"Mrs. Morris, I know this is difficult—"

The woman laughed, cutting her words off.

"That's quite an understatement. And, if you wouldn't mind terribly, I think I'd rather be known by my... by my name instead."

Wilhelmina offered her a smile. "Of course, Miss Easton."

After she was settled in, Wilhelmina stepped back out into the main room and stopped. Sitting in one of her chairs was Gabriel Shaw, holding a large envelope.

In the back of her mind, she knew she should have expected him, but she hadn't expected him to just appear in her office, especially not this late. She had been distracted dealing with Miss Easton though so perhaps he hadn't simply appeared.

"I brought the photos we spoke about." He offered her the envelope.

"Thank you."

She took it and carefully pulled the pictures out, laying them across her desk. Mrs. Rowley's face took up most of the first few photos she looked at, which wasn't surprising considering Mr. Shaw had been hired to follow her. But as she got further into the photos, she found that there were photos of the man. Blurry and grainy, it was hard to really get a clear picture of who he was.

"Do you know who he is?"

"I never followed him. Mr. Rowley wasn't paying me enough."

She nodded.

"There's some clearer pictures towards the end."

Sure enough, the next one she flipped to was a clear picture of his face. She blinked, because she wasn't sure if she was seeing something that wasn't there or not. After all, plenty of men looked similar. But it definitely was something worth exploring.

She held them up. "Has Mr. Rowley seen these?"

Mr. Shaw frowned. "Of course. I gave them to him as soon as I developed them."

She swallowed hard, looking back down at the pages.

"Why? Is something wrong?"

13

———

JAMES

Mornings were always James' favorite time of the day. The world was still quiet enough that he could have some much-needed peace. The brisk chill in the air would disappear as the sun rose in the sky, but for now, in the pre-dawn hours, he could enjoy the weather.

He had snuck into the kitchen before he left and ate a bit of the bread and jam the cook left out for him already knowing his new habit of not eating breakfast. He planned to go to the park and let Muse off of her leash and let her stretch her legs a bit before the park got too crowded. A dog off-leash would be much less welcomed when more people were there.

Weekends meant little to most of the upper-class crowds, but for James, having a few days away from writing about other people's lives was a nice reprieve. If he got up early enough, he could avoid most of the household and his uncle and sneak away before he was ever seen.

He didn't want to push, but it felt like Wilhelmina wasn't even working on Emma's case anymore. Her focus had been taken over by the divorce case he knew she had been working on before, and while he understood why, it grated at him a bit. Was Emma not as important as a divorce?

Muse whined and he scratched her ears. That was unfair of him. She had taken the other case first. Of course she would be trying to wrap up any loose ends involved in that case first.

"Poyntz!" James heard someone exclaim and he looked up. Lord Auldkirk rode up to him on horseback, stopping a short way away. He dismounted. "Out for a morning stroll?"

"Of course."

Auldkirk nodded and let Muse sniff at his gloved fingers.

"Not much use for a hunting dog here," he commented.

James snorted, but kept a firm hold on the leash.

"Never know. Maybe I should let her loose in the park and let her track some rabbits."

Auldkirk grinned, before his expression grew somber.

"Has there been any news about your cousin?"

"None yet." The wait felt like it was killing him, but he could hardly say that. Not now.

Auldkirk grabbed the reins of his horse and they walked side by side.

"Have patience. They've got to find something."

The words were hollow though. They both knew that the police would find nothing new. No, Emma would sit in prison and then go through an ordeal of a trial and then return to prison. It was a grim future to consider.

"I'm sorry. I didn't mean to bring up such an unhappy topic now."

James swallowed and nodded. "I know."

The air between them felt thick and Auldkirk glanced out at the still misty park. Soon, it would be getting crowded as more people woke up. He knew that most of the women didn't come out until later in the day when the sun was high, unless they were horseback riding or early risers. He never saw his aunt until much later in the day. Emma used to greet him at breakfast though and eating breakfast at home without her felt strange and left him in a bad mood for the rest of the day.

"Charlie talks about you."

James frowned. "She does?"

After the other night, he imagined she only would have unflattering things to say about him. It wasn't like he had been particularly sensitive to how she had been talking to him.

But Auldkirk seemed oblivious to that. "She likes your articles. Said you had a way with words."

James glanced away. A careless way with words would be more accurate. But he didn't plan to correct Auldkirk, if his sister hadn't been complaining about him. No use causing trouble. He had enough of it as it was.

"I'm actually meeting a friend this morning so I should be going."

James nodded. "Of course."

Auldkirk gave him a look he couldn't quite identify before he nodded and mounted the horse again.

***

THE WALK BACK TO HIS AUNT AND UNCLE'S HOUSE WAS as gloomy as it had been the last several days since the arrest. His mind kept flashing back to seeing all of the policemen waiting for them, like the girl, a mere child, was so dangerous it required so many people to bring her in.

He climbed the steps slowly, Muse trampling underfoot as he went. "Stop it."

She whined, before she let out a loud bark.

"Be quiet," he admonished. "You'll wake the whole street."

Not that anyone really should be asleep at this time. The sun was up and there wasn't even a cloud in the sky.

Muse fixed him with a pitiful stare as James opened the door. He shook his head and shooed the dog inside.

Mrs. Edwards glanced at them as they came in. She frowned, the phone pressed to her ear. "I'll let him know." A pause. "Thank you. You as well."

She hung up and James felt his brow furrow.

"Is something wrong?"

"Mrs. Allen asked if you were available to go to her office."

He nodded and passed Muse's leash to her. "Tell my aunt and uncle I'll be back later."

He glanced in the mirror, checking that he wasn't too rumpled from his walk, and left.

14

JAMES

James found Wilhelmina sitting at her desk studying a picture. Her desk was covered in files and papers. She didn't look up as he came into the room.

"You wanted to see me?"

She jumped slightly as she looked up. Her eyes were bloodshot and her hair messy, strands falling from her usual updo.

"Tell me I'm crazy. Tell me this isn't Simon Swinton."

He frowned and stepped behind the desk. The man in the photograph she was holding did bear a certain resemblance to Mr. Swinton.

Perhaps the woman had a reason to kill Mr. Swinton. Her face was obscured in the photos by her large hat, but she was well-dressed. Average height and nothing to really distinguish her from any other woman in London.

"Who's the woman with him?"

Wilhelmina licked her lips and blinked. Had she slept at all?

"Mrs. Eliza Rowley. My divorce client." She straightened. "You can't tell anyone that's who I'm working for."

"I won't."

He picked up another photo of the man and from a different angle. It clearly was Mr. Swinton.

"So Swinton was having an affair with a married woman?"

"It seems that way, doesn't it?"

He frowned. A married woman would have a reason to kill the man she was having an affair with. Although—

"Didn't your client want a divorce from her husband?"

"She does."

She swallowed. Mrs. Rowley wouldn't have very much reason to kill her lover if she thought she was going to get out of the marriage soon.

Wilhelmina leaned in closer and when she spoke this time, her voice was barely above a whisper, "I think the husband might have killed Mr. Swinton. He didn't want to a divorce. Her father paid them an allowance every month. An allowance that would stop if she was successful."

"Is he violent?"

She shook his head. "His wife said no. That's been part of why we needed more evidence. Her father arranged the marriage and she's been unhappy." She sighed, dropping back down into her chair. "I didn't know about this"—she gestured at the desk— "until Mr. Shaw, a private investigator that Mr. Rowley hired, told me. He's the one who took these. And he gave them to—"

She cut herself off, swaying slightly in her seat.

"I should go to his flat. Maybe there's something..."

James shook his head.

"You should get some rest. When's the last time you've slept?"

"I'm not that tired—" A yawn interrupted her. "I can't go to sleep right now."

"Why?"

The door creaked open.

He frowned as a young lady in a house dress came in. She glanced at Wilhelmina and James could see in the girl's expression that she was terrified.

"Who…?"

"This is Mrs. M—Miss Easton. Mr. Rowley's second wife."

The young woman's eyes grew wide.

"Miss Easton, this is James Poyntz, a friend."

"How do you do?"

The girl bobbed her head, but didn't speak.

Sudden horror washed over him. No wonder why Wilhelmina hadn't slept. She thought that Mr. Rowley might track down his mistress.

But she had brought Miss Easton back to Prescott House, which he doubted she would have done if she thought that he would come here.

"You should sleep," he told her seriously.

"But I can't just—"

"I'll bring her downstairs. Ezra is more than capable of watching over her. And I'm sure Mrs. Smith would be more than happy to get Miss Easton something to eat."

He looked to Miss Easton, who nodded.

"I don't mind being downstairs. My mum was a housemaid."

James smiled but it felt a bit forced. He hoped she wouldn't notice and figured Wilhelmina was too tired to notice.

"A few hours rest won't make much difference."

She nodded.

"I suppose."

It didn't take much to coax her out of the chair. He locked the office door behind them, though that wouldn't stop anyone looking to break in. He tucked her files into the spot she directed him to behind one of the loose panels surrounding the chimney. If someone was desperate enough, they would find the hiding place, but at least they weren't out in the open.

With Wilhelmina heading upstairs, James led Miss Easton to the entrance downstairs he'd been led to more than once by Thea. The staff was perhaps his favorite part of being at Prescott House. He was sure they all knew who he was a relation to the family.

"Mr. Poyntz," the butler, Mr. Morgan, greeted him, eying the young lady behind him. "What can I do for you?"

"Can Miss Easton stay down here while Mrs. Allen rests?"

"Of course, sir."

Miss Easton shuffled slightly. "I don't want to be any trouble."

"Nonsense." Mrs. Green, the housekeeper at Prescott House, smiled at Miss Easton as she approached them. "It's no trouble at all."

She gently guided Miss Easton into the kitchen and James followed. If Mrs. Smith was going to make something for the young woman, he hoped she would be willing to make something for him to eat as well.

He paused in the doorway. Lord Astermore was inside, sneaking bits of food off of the lunch trays. He caught a glimpse of James and Miss Easton and stopped, staring at them.

"Mrs. Smith, we have guests."

The cook gasped and turned.

Lord Astermore smiled at them, but there was something not quite right about the look on his face. Where had he learned to smile, because it seemed forced, like he tried practicing in a mirror one too many times rather than watching other people. "Who's this?"

"Lord Astermore, this is Miss Easton. She's part of one of Mrs. Allen's cases."

The food on the stove smelled divine.

"May we have some, Mrs. Smith?"

Miss Easton stayed quiet beside him.

The cook hesitated before she nodded. "Just not any of the lunch. And take it out of my kitchen."

"Yes, ma'am."

She huffed and turned back to the food.

"Is everything all right?" Lord Astermore asked James as he watched Miss Easton take a plate of food. "Mrs. Allen's never brought anyone involved in her cases here."

"She's taken on several cases."

Lord Astermore nodded. "Are any of them dangerous?"

James let out a breath, running his hand through his hair. "I don't know."

On the one hand, Mr. Rowley didn't seem like the kind of man to get violent. But on the other hand, he possibly killed his wife's lover.

He knew she had other cases waiting, but what they were was another question entirely. Emma's, the divorce case, his aunt's missing silver. He knew that there were other cases, but she hadn't referenced any of them.

"I don't think any of them would track her here."

He nodded slowly, but James didn't think he understood. He hadn't been around during Thea's adventures as a detective so at least he didn't know exactly how much trouble his sister had gotten into at the time. Stories could be exaggerated after the fact, and the facts had a way of being obscured with time.

"And Mrs. Allen? Will she be in any danger?"

James shook his head. "Only if she puts herself in it."

Which he had a sneaking suspicion that she would.

15

WILHELMINA

A BIT OF REST REALLY DID MAKE A WORLD OF difference. With fresh eyes on the case, Wilhelmina hoped that something would help her make some progress.

Wilhelmina guided Miss Easton into the library and closed the doors behind her.

"Can you tell me about him?"

"My husband?" the young woman asked uncertainly.

Wilhelmina nodded.

"What would you like to know?"

Wilhelmina motioned to the couches and they both sat. Miss Easton shifted nervously, rearranging her skirts around her just so she would have something to do that didn't involve looking at Wilhelmina, it seemed.

"I heard you earlier," she said, her voice so quiet Wilhelmina could barely hear her. "You think he killed someone."

She sighed. There was no point lying about it if she overheard her. "I do."

"He's not a murderer. He's kind and never been violent."

Wilhelmina didn't want to point out that Miss Easton wasn't

exactly the best judge in Mr. Rowley's character, considering he had been married at the time that he had married her.

"Someone doesn't necessarily have to be violent to kill someone."

If that was the case, poison wouldn't be such a popular choice for killing people. It was so simple to use, almost like they didn't actually do anything to the person. Just slip something into their drink or their food and sooner or later, they would be dead. It certainly wouldn't have captured the imagination of so many authors and been continually used for centuries as a way to get rid of husbands and enemies alike.

Wilhelmina shifted and let out a breath. "Does he have any medicines?"

She shook her head. "He's always been very healthy." Miss Easton frowned. "Oh! About a month ago, the doctor did prescribe him laurel water because he's been having trouble sleeping."

"Laurel water?"

She nodded. "That's not dangerous though, is it? I'm sure plenty of people have trouble sleeping."

They did, but it was interesting that he was prescribed the same substance that the police thought Mr. Swinton was killed with.

Even though Miss Easton was upset the night before, she seemed almost defensive of Mr. Rowley. It was like she forgot that the man lied to her for a year.

"You're right." She offered Miss Easton a smile. "If you don't mind, I'd like to look around your flat though. Even if Mr. Morris didn't kill Mr. Swinton, he might know who might have, since they knew each other."

She nodded. "I know you think I must be foolish to believe in him, but what he and I share together is real. I know he loves me."

Wilhelmina hesitated at the devotion in the girl's face. It was strange to think that she felt that way, even in the face of so much evidence proving that the man was a liar. But then again, how easy was it to dismiss that kind of behavior. She had done it for years, telling herself that Ernest didn't really mean to hurt her or cheat on her or come home drunk. She had tried to change herself to fit his image of a perfect woman and told herself she failed when she hadn't and had managed to convince herself that it was her fault.

It would take time for Miss Easton to see Mr. Rowley as he really was, if she ever saw him that way.

In lieu of an answer, she offered Miss Easton a smile.

"WELL?" JAMES ASKED AS HE STOOD IN THE ENTRANCE hall.

"She doesn't think he did it." Wilhelmina glanced back and lowered her voice. "Not that I'm surprised."

James grimaced. "I'd stay and help, but I have to go to work."

Wilhelmina shook her head. "It's fine."

"You'll let me know if you need anything, won't you?"

"Of course." She smiled. She wasn't going to tell him that she had no plans of doing so. She could handle herself just fine.

He bowed his head and walked out the door. Wilhelmina waited until he was gone from sight before she pulled on her jacket and hat.

Mr. Rowley's secret flat wasn't far and it would be easy enough to walk there. He told Miss Easton that he wouldn't be home for a couple of days so the flat should be empty and she could take a look around with no problems.

It was probably incredibly stupid to break in somewhere where she suspected a murderer to live. But Miss Easton had given her the key to the flat so it wasn't really breaking in. As long as she didn't leave a trace that she was there, he shouldn't be any wiser.

Wilhelmina had deliberately picked out an outfit that matched Miss Easton's wardrobe. They were shaped a bit differently.

Wilhelmina was significantly taller than Miss Easton, but she could dress enough like her. No one would notice if a woman sort of matching Miss Easton's general looks walked into her own flat, especially if she had a key. All she had to do was walk in, take a look around, and then get out of there. She had no issues with telling Inspector Haddington about whatever she found.

She listened inside the flat. She couldn't hear anyone moving around in there, so she figured it was safe enough. She slipped the key in the door and it opened without a problem.

"Hello?" she called out and was relieved when no one answered.

She shut the door behind her.

Everything was so still, so quiet, and she wasn't sure where to begin. Where would one hide poison?

Except... except, it wasn't really poison, was it? Or, at least, it wasn't intended as poison. It was intended as medicine. Medicine intended to help him sleep. If it was her, she would keep it by her bedside, or at least in the bedroom.

The bedroom was tidy for a household without a maid. Everything had its place and it would be very clear if she had to ruffle around in their possessions. Fortunately though, she didn't have to. On the vanity, there was a bottle of hydrocyanic acid. Cyanide, just like what had killed Mr. Swinton.

She needed to show it to the police. If Inspector Haddington saw it... but there was no proof it was here in his apartment.

The front door creaked open.

16

WILHELMINA

WILHELMINA'S HEART HAMMERED IN HER CHEST. As carefully as she could, she put the bottle back exactly as she found it and pressed herself against the wall, mindful of where she stepped. One wrong move would be all that was needed to alert Mr. Rowley that someone was here when they shouldn't be.

Something squeaked in the sitting room. She heard him opening a cabinet in the other room and winced. Her best bet would be to leave through the bedroom window, but she wouldn't be able to lock the window and surely he would notice. She couldn't do anything to make him suspicious.

A knock on the front door came a moment later.

"Ah, Shaw."

What was he doing there?

"Did you find something for me?"

"Nothing much, sir."

The door closed.

"Then why are you here, Shaw?"

"You told me to keep you informed."

Wilhelmina risked a glance out the door and into the hallway. The window in the sitting room was open... Mr. Rowley must have opened it when he came in. It was just enough that she thought she could get out, that was if Shaw kept him distracted for long enough.

"I found out who was following you. Some lady detective. Mrs. Rowley hired her to get pictures of you. She wasn't that invested in the whole thing."

"Really? That's surprising."

"You know how these lady detectives are," Shaw said dismissively as she crept closer to where they were. "They're in it for a bit of excitement. Not really in it for the work."

"Mmm. That's quite true," Mr. Rowley agreed. "I always say that a woman's place is in the home."

Shaw shot her a look while Rowley was distracted with his drink and Wilhelmina took the chance to dart across the room with silent steps. It seemed that her youthful days of sneaking out of her grandparents' house had come in handy for something.

"I couldn't agree more with you."

"So what did this woman have? Anything?"

"Said she hadn't been able to get anything. But she said Mrs. Rowley only hired her after the last detective botched the job—"

She didn't hear the rest as she slipped through the window. It was fortunate for her that whoever constructed the building made it in such a way that it was easy enough to climb down, even in a long skirt. One wrong move and she would slip. If she didn't get herself killed by falling, she would definitely alert Mr. Rowley with the noise.

She clung on to each stone and felt with her boot for the next spot before she moved from the one she was on.

"Don't look down," she muttered to herself.

It was better to close her eyes than look down. If she looked, she would fall for sure.

The next ledge turned out to be the ground and she let out a huff of relief as she landed. With any luck, Shaw would come out soon. She needed to tell Inspector Haddington about the bottle, but even with motive and means, she feared he wouldn't be able to do anything. Even a confession wasn't always enough for the police when they already had a suspect.

No, in order to clear Emma, the case would have to be airtight.

And then she could finally focus on the missing spoons and Thea's comb. The fact that James thought Thea and Inspector Thayne were married was laughable, but they were no doubt heading towards it. Though clearly nothing had been made official or else Lady Astermore would stop arranging so many dinner partners. It was only her relatively recent widowhood that spared Wilhelmina from Lady Astermore's matchmaking efforts.

Perhaps Mrs. Rowley would know something more. She had been married to Mr. Rowley for a number of years before she decided to seek a divorce. She would never be compelled to testify against him and the police wouldn't be able to do anything with any information Mrs. Rowley gave, but perhaps it would give Wilhelmina a starting point for building something she could give the police.

After all, a man didn't just wake up one day and decide to poison someone, let alone at someone else's house. No... it had been deliberate. There would be signs, something that would have shown his intent leading up to that. Between getting the laurel water weeks in advance and the fact that the murder was committed in such a way that wouldn't directly trace back to him, it was clear that he had planned it.

Finally, Shaw walked out of the building. He glanced around before he made his way discreetly across the street to where he saw her waiting.

"How did you know I was in there?"

He grinned. "I've been following you, haven't I? Saw you go in, then him. Figured you might need a distraction."

She took a breath. Could she trust him? He could have told Mr. Rowley that she was there, or who she was, or where he could find her. To the best of her knowledge, he didn't do any of that.

"Why did you help me?"

Few people helped anyone without knowing that they would gain something in return. It just wasn't the way of the world. She had learned very young from her grandfather that altruistic acts were usually a cover up for something else, and she didn't know Shaw well enough to say he wasn't looking for something from her.

"Why not help?" He shrugged. "We're in the same line of work. Sooner or later, we might see each other again."

So he might want something in the future. She could understand that. He wouldn't be the first person she had met since becoming a detective that offered help once only to collect on that favor at a later date.

She smiled at him. "Thank you. I appreciate it."

"You have my card. If you need any assistance, don't hesitate." He bowed his head ever so slightly. "It's been a pleasure, Mrs. Allen."

17

———

JAMES

"You did what?!"

James pinched the bridge of his nose, feeling his head throb. Nothing about it made sense.

"It was a calculated risk," Wilhelmina said as she crossed her arms defensively and glared down at him. "I wasn't in any danger."

He knew that was a lie.

"And I already told Inspector Haddington."

That was something at least. Thea would have been reluctant to do that much. But this wasn't a hobby for Wilhelmina. This was her livelihood so it made sense that she would have to think about it differently.

Still, he said, "You're not a policeman. You shouldn't be risking your life like that."

Wilhelmina glared. "You hired me to find out who did it. I have a solid, credible lead for that, one that I intend to follow up on and see if he actually killed Mr. Swinton."

He gritted his teeth. It wouldn't be worth arguing with her.

Thea looked up from where she was sitting on the terrace when he walked out. She frowned as she saw him, her eyes narrowing and her brow furrowing, but she thankfully did not ask him what was wrong or if he was all right. Instead, she closed her book and stood.

"Let's go for a walk."

Thea led him through the house without a word. She set her book on the front table as she passed it and pulled on her jacket and hat.

"Won't you be missed?" James finally asked.

"Maybe." She tilted her head. "Maybe not. Mother's been... occupied." She glanced at him quickly before she looked away again. "With Colonel Bantry."

James winced. He knew that but it was still strange to hear it.

"Your brother and sister-in-law?"

Thea raised her brows as she opened the door.

"*Our* brother and sister-in-law," she corrected with a teasing smile. "Ilene is visiting people today and Cecil is somewhere. Probably at the club."

Despite having all those people in Prescott House, Thea always seemed rather lonely. It certainly explained a lot about her and why she had been so willing to accept him as quickly as she had.

She led him down the street towards one of the parks. He couldn't help but wonder how they looked from an outsider's perspective. Did they look like two mismatched people taking a stroll? Two casual acquaintances who happened to meet?

"I feel like I'm losing my mind," he admitted, shoving his hands in his pockets to keep himself from running them through his hair. "I feel useless to help her... Emma," he clarified. "Wilhelmina runs off into danger and I'm stuck, unable to do anything to help her."

"Have you been to see her?"

He shook her head. "They won't let me in." He kicked at the

ground and when he spoke again, resentment bled into his words. "If I was her brother, I could get in."

When he was younger, he used to wish his aunt and uncle had formally adopted him when his parents died, so that he was their child in the eyes of the law and not just their ward. It would have made things so much easier.

Emma had been the only one who had made him feel like he belonged. He knew his aunt and uncle didn't do it on purpose, but his childhood had been isolating in a way. Even if he had been his parents, Arthur and Lucy's son, he still wouldn't have been Uncle Neville and Aunt Helen's child. Only their ward.

He let out a breath.

Thea reached for his hand and he let her pull it from his pocket and squeeze it. Thea wasn't very tactile and shows of affection didn't come easily for her. She was more like her cat than she would ever care to admit, a bit distant and cold at times but never truly unfriendly. It was like she was as afraid as he was.

"We can talk to Inspector Thayne," she said. "Perhaps he can help you get in."

James shook his head. He didn't want to deal with false hope and he already knew there was nothing that could be done.

"Speaking of Inspector Thayne, I heard he gave you a comb for Christmas."

Her cheeks flushed bright red.

"I'm surprised you didn't elope with him so Lady Astermore would stop her matchmaking attempts."

Thea's eyes narrowed.

"I thought about it," she muttered under her breath. "Do you know that she's attempted to match me with her brother Colin multiple times?"

Thea shook her head.

"My grandmother is worse." She looked at him. "Actually our grandmother, the American one, is by far worse."

James frowned, but Thea continued on, getting more animated as she went.

"Louise Craven... that's our grandmother's name," she said, giving him a smile. "Louisa was my great-grandmother's name. The Dowager Countess' mother. The fact that Ilene named the new baby Louisa must be driving her mad."

James glanced at her. "Cecil didn't name her?"

Thea laughed and he was taken aback for a moment. It seemed like her laughter was a rare thing. She tended to be so serious about everything. "Cecil never names anything."

He blinked and they continued through the park. Somehow, she had managed to change the subject and he hadn't even noticed.

"So, how is the Dowager Countess worse?"

"She just... I think she's why Ilene keeps trying to play match-maker. The man she tried to set me up with at Christmas was older than my mother."

James blinked again.

"She and mother hate each other. When we moved into Prescott House permanently, it was under the condition that my grandmother could never stay there." Thea glanced away. "She wouldn't like Leslie. A second son... a baron's second son at that. No title, no real inheritance. She wants me to marry, but she also wants someone who will improve my standing in society."

He caught a glimpse at her face.

"That's why she and our American grandmother don't get along. They're both very similar. Mother's mother... she was a poor Irish immigrant. She had nothing and went to America and married well. Then she expected Mother to marry well too. Cousin Stella is the oldest granddaughter and she married an earl. As an earl's daughter, she has even higher expectations for me."

James looked at her. "That's a lot to expect of you."

"But at least she never comes over here. Says the climate doesn't agree with her."

James laughed. "Have you been to America?"

Thea shook her head. "I thought about it." She glanced away. "Aunt Dot said she'd take me. Mother didn't want me to go alone. But then..."

She trailed off, but it didn't matter. He knew how that sentence would have ended anyway.

"I've been before, on assignments." He smiled. "Wilhelmina has too. I bet between the two of us, we could probably keep you out of too much trouble."

Thea laughed again and James felt himself grin in response.

"I don't think Mother would agree. Wilhelmina's in constant trouble anymore, especially with her business."

James shook his head. She didn't even know the half of it. What would Thea have thought about Wilhelmina running head-first into the danger, breaking into a possible murderer's flat? A smile played on his lips. Thea probably would have done the same last year.

"Let's get something to eat," she said with a smile.

18

——————

JAMES

With Wilhelmina focusing on Emma's case, it couldn't hurt to work on trying to find Thea's comb. After all, James had been at two of the parties where things had gone missing. He liked to think of it as lending his perspective or so he told himself as he sorted through old newspapers. Wilhelmina would be annoyed to accept help, but it was his aunt's things that had been stolen. He benefited from looking for them.

"Are you looking for something specific?" Henry Phillips asked and James looked up.

He had almost forgotten that he had commandeered Phillips' desk to look through the photos he had taken at the parties. The last time he looked through them he had only been looking for Mr. Swinton. Now, he suspected there was far more to this than just the death.

And Henry Phillips seemed to have been the only one to put it together. The police had barely bothered. James thought he had heard that they arrested a maid at one of the houses and a footman at another but the thefts hadn't stopped.

"Yes, but I'm not sure what." James flipped through the pages. "Isn't there more?"

Phillips shook his head. "I stopped writing about it. Mr. Watson"—the editor of the West End Gazette—"thought that this was too likely to cause panic in our readers."

"But you've gone to the parties since, haven't you?"

Phillips nodded.

"Have you seen anything?"

He nodded. "The thefts didn't stop." He glanced down, shuffling the papers. "But I didn't take many pictures. Mr. Watson said I was wasting film and anymore not related to the story would come out of my paycheck."

James wished he could march into Mr. Watson's office and yell at him. He probably could, but he didn't want to deal with the questions and he wasn't entirely sure that his uncle knew that things were missing from their house. After all, his aunt had hired Wilhelmina for discretion. She wouldn't appreciate him shouting their business for the world to hear.

"If I knew who you were looking for—"

"The thief," James hissed, glancing around. "I want to know who's behind this."

Phillips brightened. "Oh! There's a few people, I think. They work together."

That made sense. Then they could trade out. They only needed to have an alibi for whenever they were the one stealing. It also would allow them to cover more houses without being too suspicious. If the same person was always found in places they shouldn't be, then of course they would be caught. But one person wandering through the house wasn't as suspicious.

"Are they temporary staff then?"

Phillips shook his head. "I don't think so. The staff was questioned by the police in both cases where they arrested someone for the missing items and they never saw anything. I think they're guests."

WITH THE NEW POSSIBILITIES SPINNING IN HIS HEAD, James left the office and headed to Prescott House. Wilhelmina wasn't in her office. He frowned, though that wasn't too particular. However, he had an uneasiness that had refused to leave him all day. Something wasn't quite right and he wasn't entirely sure what that was.

Flipping through Wilhelmina's case notes on the thefts, James couldn't help but notice the names that repeated. She had been looking for evidence of Mr. Rowley's affair, but there was so much more than that here.

He had the sneaking suspicion that one of the thieves was Mrs. Rowley, Wilhelmina's client. It made sense. She would lose her inheritance when she divorced her husband. Mr. Swinton had probably been among their number as well. Without her inheritance, they would have been poor and selling off the items they stole would go a long way in helping to maintain Mrs. Rowley's lifestyle. Mr. Swinton hadn't been from the richest of families and from what James had seen, Mrs. Rowley did have expensive tastes.

The Rowley's house wasn't far. He didn't exactly have a plan. It wasn't like he could barge in there and accuse her of stealing. But he needed to know if she had been behind it. Being able to recover some of the items would be a small comfort to his aunt, especially if she was lying to his uncle about it.

He caught a glimpse through one of the windows of a familiar hat. Wilhelmina was there? Had she found something else?

James walked up to the door quietly, frowning as he noticed the way the door wasn't quite closed. That didn't make any sense for a house like this. He laid his hand flat against the door and pushed it open.

19

WILHELMINA

WILHELMINA DEBATED WITH HERSELF FOR A WHILE before she left Prescott House that morning. On the one hand, it would be rude to drop by unannounced and unexpected, but on the other hand, Mrs. Rowley could know something about her husband's activities. The police wouldn't be able to act on that knowledge, but there was nothing that would stop her from acting on the knowledge. It was fortunate that she wasn't tied to any such constraints.

"Mrs. Allen," Mrs. Rowley greeted as Wilhelmina entered the sitting room. "I hadn't expected you today."

Mrs. Rowley was alone, thankfully. Part of her thought that Mr. Rowley might go home, since he had told Miss Easton that he wouldn't be at their flat. But he had come back there so it was hard to actually predict where he would be at any given day.

"Is your husband home?"

Mrs. Rowley stared at her, her expression darkening. "No. He's not welcome back here either." She straightened and for a moment Wilhelmina was reminded that Mrs. Rowley had been raised a baron's daughter. "I've given my butler specific instructions not to let him in."

Not that it would really stop him if he wanted to get in. He was still her husband and this was still his home. Wilhelmina could only hope that the staff was loyal to Mrs. Rowley over Mr. Rowley.

"I was hoping to ask you about him."

Mrs. Rowley motioned for her to sit.

"His other—" Wilhelmina cut herself off. "Miss Easton said he was taking laurel water and that he hadn't been able to sleep."

Mrs. Rowley snorted. "I hope he can't sleep."

"Does he have that here as well?"

She shook her head. "Never. He's always been rather healthy. If he has trouble sleeping, I'd never know." Mrs. Rowley leaned in. "We haven't shared a bed in years."

"What about Mr. Swinton?"

Mrs. Rowley went pale. "You knew?"

Wilhelmina nodded. "Mr. Rowley had an investigator following you. There are photos."

Her hand rested on her stomach and Wilhelmina's eyes followed the movement. There was nothing that gave her away specifically, just a feeling, but somehow, Wilhelmina knew. After living with Molly in the household for the past year, it was almost obvious.

"Mrs. Rowley, I have to ask. Are you...?"

"Expecting?" she asked, her voice barely a whisper. She nodded. "I found out shortly before Simon's death."

"Is it...?"

"It's Simon's." The color still hadn't returned to her face. "That's why I need the divorce now more than ever. If I don't, Robert can... Robert will..."

Wilhelmina didn't need her to finish the sentence. Mr. Robert would claim the child as his own.

"Simon and I were going to get married and go away for a while. Then it would be harder for Robert to prove when..."

Wilhelmina nodded.

"He can still claim the child even if the divorce goes through now."

The court would take the child away too, especially with the proof that she had committed adultery. The only way for her to keep her child now would be to go away indefinitely or to remarry immediately.

"Do you think he knows about your condition?"

Mrs. Rowley grew still.

"Oh no…" She stared at Wilhelmina. "I think he does."

"When do you think he found out?"

Mrs. Rowley stared up at her with undisguised horror in her eyes. Her lips moved silently and Wilhelmina wished that she could read lips. Still she didn't need to hear the words to know that it was before Mr. Swinton's death that Mr. Rowley found out.

Suddenly her eyes darted behind Wilhelmina and dread settled in her stomach. She couldn't explain it—the tightness in her chest, the way her heart seemed to beat faster—but she knew. Instinct, perhaps? A response learned from the years she had spent anticipating Ernest's presence.

She should have known better than to sit with her back to the door after all this time. She had gotten too complacent at Prescott House, felt too comfortable and safe. Her hands clenched in her skirt and Wilhelmina glanced around the room. The tea service was too delicate to be much use and the tea was hardly boiling. The fireplace pokers were too far away. She looked up.

Mr. Rowley's reflection glared at her in the glass of the framed photographs sitting on the mantle.

20

WILHELMINA

"WHAT ARE YOU DOING IN MY HOUSE?" MR. ROWLEY demanded.

Wilhelmina took a breath, standing up slowly as she kept her hands where he could see them. She didn't want him to think she was going to attack him, but she also wanted to get as much distance between them as she could. He was too close and her throat felt too tight near him.

She wasn't going to be weak again. What was the point of learning Ju-Jitsu if she was going to be helpless at the first sign of danger. There was nothing to say that Mr. Rowley would attack her.

There was though. The anger in his eyes, a dark glint. He used poison to kill Mr. Swinton, but that didn't mean he couldn't physically overpower her. And Mrs. Rowley was in a delicate condition. An attack on her could prove even more dangerous. Wilhelmina was used to a bit of violence. She would heal.

"Stop moving," he ordered.

Wilhelmina swallowed hard as she froze.

"Why are you here?"

"I invited her for tea."

Mrs. Rowley's tone was soft and gentle and Wilhelmina wouldn't have known how nervous she was if she couldn't see her face out of the corner of her eye. It was obvious it was a lie. She was still wearing her gloves, which she would have taken off if she was actually having tea. There was only one cup and saucer on the tray. One plate of sandwiches.

She could tell from his gaze that he had noticed that too.

"I didn't know you were going to be home today," Mrs. Rowley continued.

He knew who she was, her gut told her. The way he was looking at her, watching her. Somehow, he knew. Shaw said he didn't show him the pictures, but she had only just met Shaw. Who was to say she could trust him?

And she doubted Mr. Rowley would threaten women he didn't know just for being in his house having tea with his wife. Even Ernest hadn't been so irrational, despite how unpredictable he had been. Certain appearances had to be kept up and having people over for tea was keeping up appearances.

"I know you've been following me," Rowley said.

Wilhelmina bit her tongue. Perhaps Shaw wasn't to blame at all. She had been sloppy, had let her guard down.

"I saw you the other day."

He took a step forward.

"Why were you following me?"

"You killed Simon Swinton."

In retrospect, this perhaps wasn't the smartest thing to say. But she wanted to keep his attention away from Mrs. Rowley. The more he focused on Wilhelmina, the better.

Still, it wasn't the expected answer, it seemed. He paused for a moment.

"I heard that girl killed him. The one the police arrested."

"She was framed. But you already knew that," Wilhelmina said. "You poisoned his drink with laurel water. He didn't die right away, which meant he wasn't near you when he died. That made it harder to prove it was you that did it. And since the police already have a suspect in custody, you knew they weren't planning on looking for another."

Mr. Rowley grinned. It wasn't a very nice grin, all teeth and anger. He looked like a wild animal. A feral creature ready to attack at any moment.

"He deserved to die," he snarled. "What kind of man carries on with another man's wife?"

"What kind of man has two wives?"

Mr. Rowley darted towards her. Wilhelmina grabbed the teapot and threw it at him. It crashed against his head and he screamed, staggering back.

"Run!" she shouted at the other woman.

Mrs. Rowley didn't hesitate. She took off through the doors.

Please be getting help, Wilhelmina prayed.

"You're going to pay for that."

She ran for the fireplace and grabbed the poker. She swung it at him but he grabbed the end. He yanked it from her hands and she cried out.

She should have gotten more training. A few moments where it actually mattered and the little she learned flew from her head.

"You think you know anything?" His face was twisted up in a snarl. "My parents forced me to marry that ungrateful shrew. My inheritance is tied up in this whole charade. If she leaves, I get nothing!"

His hand slammed into the wall near her head. She flinched.

"Does that sound fair? I put all these years in, for that. Then that man comes and thinks—"

She kneed him between the legs and darted past him. His nail caught her chin as he slammed her into the wall. She heard something thud hard. Her chin stung.

His hand gripped her throat. Her pulse throbbed in her neck as he tightened his hold. Wilhelmina reached up, digging her fingers into his hand. Why hadn't she taken off her gloves? Her nails would have been much more useful.

She lifted her foot up and slammed her boot as hard as she could into his foot.

He yelped. His grip grew tighter.

Spots dotted her vision. She needed to get loose before…

His feet weren't under hers and each movement made his grip grow tighter.

"Stay still, you—"

Porcelain shattered around them. Wilhelmina shrieked and closed her eyes against the spray of the shards. Mr. Rowley crumpled. His hand fell away.

James stood before her and Wilhelmina launched herself into his arms in relief.

21

————

JAMES

JAMES WRAPPED HIS ARMS AROUND WILHELMINA AS SHE trembled against him. He didn't like how she was wheezing. He led her to the couch and pulled off his coat, wrapping it around her.

Her hat was crushed and he felt blindly for the pins he knew kept it attached to her head, tugging them loose until the hat came off. He set it on the couch beside her.

"Is he dead?" a woman asked from the doorway. He vaguely recognized Mrs. Rowley from the photographs in Wilhelmina's office. She didn't look nearly as put together as she did in the photos.

He hadn't realized an audience had gathered. An older man who had to be the butler, a stern-faced woman who was probably the housekeeper, and a few maids in the back, peeking over.

He followed their gazes down to the floor. Mr. Rowley was still, but after a moment, his back rose and fell.

James kicked the poker away from the other man's reach.

"He's alive." He glanced around the room. "Do you have any rope? Or something I can use to tie him?"

Mrs. Rowley nodded and the butler disappeared, returning a few moments later with a belt. "Will this do, sir?"

James nodded. The butler took the poker as James knelt and tied Mr. Rowley's hands together. He hoped the man wouldn't wake up soon. He didn't imagine he would be too pleased to realize what had happened.

James stood back up and looked at Wilhelmina. She gripped his jacket with her hands, but she had stopped shaking and color had returned to her face.

"I phoned the police," Mrs. Rowley told them. "They should be here shortly."

<hr>

AMONG THE POLICE OFFICERS THAT SHOWED UP TO THE Rowley's house, Inspector Haddington was among them. He frowned as he saw Wilhelmina, his brow crinkling and eyes filling with worry.

"Is she all right?" the inspector asked.

James nodded. "She needs a doctor. He had his hand around her throat when I came in."

Inspector Haddington glowered at Mr. Rowley, who had since woken up, though James was glad to see the man had enough sense not to attempt to escape before the police arrived. With more people around, it was far less likely to go how Rowley hoped.

Wilhelmina stood and walked to them.

"He confessed." Her voice was raw and James winced. Red marks lined her throat, peeking over the top of her collar. "He killed Mr. Swinton."

Inspector Haddington glanced toward Rowley. "I'm sure the explanation makes much more sense than your cousin killing him.

James chuckled darkly. There weren't many things that made as little sense as a young lady murdering someone that she barely knew and had no motive to kill.

"I'm sure once we talk to Mr. Rowley, we can get your cousin released."

James offered his hand to the inspector and the inspector shook it. "Thank you."

The inspector eyed Wilhelmina's neck. "We'll need to get a statement from you. When you're feeling better, of course."

She smiled but it barely lifted the corners of her lips, and nodded ever so slightly.

"I'm fine," she rasped.

The inspector raised a skeptical brow. "I'm sure."

"And if that's all, I'm taking you back to Prescott House," James told her, taking her elbow with a gentle hand.

The inspector nodded and gestured at the others to let them pass.

"Will Wilhelmina be alright?" Vivien asked him as James came down the stairs. He had taken her to the second floor but she had refused his help going any further.

"A few days rest and she should be fine."

"I've called for the doctor."

James nodded.

"Will you stay for dinner?"

His mother's expression was unusually hopeful. For the first time in a long time, he found himself yearning for them to be closer. Perhaps that was why he nodded.

"Cecil and Ilene are out tonight so it'll be much more informal than it's been."

James smiled and thanked her. An informal evening suited him much better than the stiff and awkward dinners with his brother and sister-in-law.

He nearly tripped over his feet at the thought.

After dinner, he joined Thea in the library. Thea watched him in a way that matched the kitten curled up on the chair. Mercury had grown quite a bit in the last few months. He no longer resembled the tiny black kitten Thea had found in the ruins at Ravenholm Castle.

"What happened this afternoon?"

James sat. "Wilhelmina solved Mr. Swinton's murder. She was protecting someone else and got hurt, but she'll be on her feet in a few days."

"That's a relief."

She relaxed in her seat, her fingers running over the page.

He was glad she wasn't running into danger anymore. What would he do if she got hurt? Wilhelmina had trained for being in more dangerous situations and still had been injured today. Would Thea have been able to fight off Mr. Rowley?

"I'm going to Wraughtley Hall," Thea said suddenly.

James blinked.

"Wraughtley Hall?"

He knew the name, in a vague sort of way, but he wasn't sure why she was telling him?

"I want you to come with me."

He frowned.

"I don't know the... the Wraughtleys?" What an absolutely dreadful name.

Thea laughed and he hoped it wasn't because of his expression. "You don't know them *yet*."

"I'm not sure that's such a good idea." Showing up to people's houses unexpected usually wasn't. After all the trouble in the past few weeks, the last thing he wanted was to invite more trouble.

"The Countess of Wraughtley, Stella Pemberton, is our cousin."

"Pemberton..." He could have smacked himself. He knew the name sounded familiar. "She married William Pemberton. We went to school together," he added at Thea's curious glance.

She blinked, then grinned.

"Then you already know William. Stella's wanted to meet you for a while."

Why couldn't they meet there in London? It seemed strange to meet someone for the first time in their home. Although, the fact that he went to school with Pemberton did make it less odd.

"We both thought you might like to go out to the country and get away."

"It might be nice," he said and took a breath. "Can I have some time to think about it before I agree?"

She smiled. "Of course."

"When do you leave?"

She glanced back towards the door. "Next week."

He nodded. "I'll let you know in the next few days."

He smiled at her before he turned and walked out the doors. The hallway was quieter, but he didn't allow himself to stop until he had said goodnight and smiled and pretended every-thing was all right. It wasn't until James stepped outside the house into the now-cooler night air that he allowed himself to think.

He would have to tell his aunt and uncle. They wouldn't be likely to let Emma go with him, not after this. He couldn't blame them. They had all been through an ordeal, but the result had left him feeling more like an outsider than usual. Maybe it would be good to get away.

***

"I CAN'T BELIEVE YOU'RE GOING TO BE LEAVING already. I've barely been home a week," Emma complained as she clung to his bedpost, watching him fold his clothes into his trunk. The old silver bracelet on her wrist sparkled in the flicker of the gaslight.

He gave her a smile that he hoped came across as reassuring.

"It won't be a long trip. And it's not too far so it'll be easy enough to come back. Or I'm sure Lord and Lady Wraughtley wouldn't be opposed to you joining us."

Emma snorted in a positively unladylike fashion that would have gotten her a scolding if her mother had witnessed it. Although, after what she had been through, perhaps it wouldn't have.

"As if Mother and Father are ever letting me out of their sight again," she groaned.

He laughed.

Downstairs, he could hear people on the street and the door open.

Emma let go of the bed and bounced to the window.

"That'll be the Ravenholms."

His aunt and uncle had invited them for dinner. 'Some normalcy for Emma,' they had said. It would be good for her to see her friend, even if it would be a bit awkward with the way Lady Charlotte refused to meet his eyes anymore.

She leaned against the glass. "Scotland's a long way away. You don't suppose Lord Auldkirk would be willing to marry me so I could go, do you?"

James shook his head. Somehow, he very much doubted that Auldkirk thought of Emma as anything beyond his sister's friend. But he wouldn't be the one to tell Emma that.

"Come on. We should go greet them. You could finish packing later."

Something white on his desk caught his eye. James shook his head again as she tried to pull him from the room. "I'll be down in just a minute."

Emma let out a huff and let go, marching out the door as dramatically as she could.

With everything that had gone on, James had forgotten about the files of old newspapers and the police report he had asked Thayne for. Being away from London seemed like a good time to read them and gain a bit of clarity on the situation. The last thing he wanted to do was to rush into investigating two deaths that took place years ago without any background.

He wasn't sure they were actually murdered, but if Thea thought they were, it was worth looking into, if for no other reason than to put her fears to rest.

He tucked the files into his briefcase, closed the latches, and went downstairs to join their guests for dinner.

22

WILHELMINA

There was no reason to be nervous, Wilhelmina told herself.

Just because the last time she was in that flat, she had to climb out of a window didn't mean that she needed to be nervous. Mr. Rowley was gone, had been arrested, and Emma had been released. He couldn't hurt her.

And yet...

Wilhelmina rubbed at her throat. It didn't hurt anymore, not really, but she had woken a number of times in the middle of the night imagining his hand around her neck again. It would be a long time before the nightmares stopped.

Miss Easton shuffled around the apartment. Most of the surfaces were bare. Her things were in the process of being packed. Anything not packed would soon be auctioned off by Mr. Rowley's parents. Both were most displeased at their son's behavior. He had been disowned, but best of all, Mrs. Rowley had been granted a divorce, as had Miss Easton. The Rowleys had been kind to Miss Easton though and allowed her to keep some of what Robert had bought her. *It wasn't her fault that Robert deceived her,* the Rowleys had said. It was far more kindness than the

Livingstons had extended to Wilhelmina in the wake of Ernest's death.

"I didn't know," Miss Easton sighed as she pulled a framed bit of embroidery from the walls. "I should have known. He was too good to be true."

She leaned her head against the door frame.

"Does she hate me? Mrs. Rowley?"

Wilhelmina shook her head. "I don't think so. She's asked about meeting you."

Miss Easton turned her head. "When?"

"Today?"

She nodded. "I'll go get ready."

"I know this has been a hard experience, but you'll get through it."

Wilhelmina couldn't explain it, but something about Miss Easton reminded her of how she had been. She would overcome this.

"Thank you. For everything." She straightened up. "You didn't have to help me. That wasn't part of your job. But I'm very grateful that you did."

Miss Easton smiled at her, turned, and left the room.

MISS EASTON PLAYED NERVOUSLY WITH HER HAT AS they waited for the butler to open the door.

"You look fine," Wilhelmina told her and the young lady clapped her hands nervously to her side.

The door opened and the butler greeted them and let them inside. He guided them into the parlor.

"Mrs. Rowley will be down in a moment."

Wilhelmina bowed her head. "Thank you."

Miss Easton bit her lip as she glanced around the room. The parlor was a beautiful room, but cold. Wilhelmina had noticed that on her previous visits. Unlike the parlor at Prescott House, there was a coldness to it. It didn't feel like someone actually lived there, but just wanted people to think they did.

"Mrs. Allen. Thank you for coming," Mrs. Rowley greeted from the doorway.

Miss Easton turned and her eyes grew wide.

"And you must be Miss Easton."

She offered her hand and Miss Easton took it. "Hester, please."

Mrs. Rowley smiled. "Eliza." She motioned to the couch. "Shall we sit?"

Miss Easton nodded nervously.

"I feel as if I should apologize for Robert. We weren't happy long before he brought you into our mess."

"I didn't know he was married, I swear," Miss Easton told her. "I never would have... not if I had known. I'm so sorry."

Miss Easton was a sweet girl, so different from most of the mistresses that Wilhelmina had encountered during her other investigations. So different from Ernest's mistresses.

The butler brought refreshments in and Wilhelmina sipped carefully, thankful for her hands to have something to do. She watched the two of them interact and waited.

She couldn't picture herself ever entertaining her late husband's mistresses or being able to treat them with the kind of respect that Mrs. Rowley was treating Miss Easton. She wished she could be as generous, that she would have wanted to extend them a home to them if she had one, but she wouldn't have been. She resented them. They had been able to walk away, where she had been stuck. She still felt stuck, his ghost lingering over her even though it had been almost a year. When would she be free from him?

Her fingers brushed at her neck.

She wasn't the same woman she had been with him. It was time to stop letting him control her life.

"Mrs. Allen!" Mrs. Rowley called as Wilhelmina pulled on her gloves and made herself presentable to leave. "A moment, please."

Wilhelmina paused and looked at her. Mrs. Rowley motioned for her to follow and led her up the staircase and into another room.

"Simon and I took things from the parties we went to. His family wasn't well off, not anymore, and mine would have disowned me if I had left Robert."

"So you stole to make sure you'd have money after."

Mrs. Rowley nodded. "We sold most of the things we took before he..." She swallowed. "I didn't want to be caught with anything and I couldn't stay with Robert. Not..."

Her hand rested against her stomach.

"I was going to sell this. I tried to only take things that wouldn't be missed." She held out a sparkling diamond comb. Wilhelmina had never seen it before but she knew it immediately. "Something about this... I don't know what it was, but I couldn't bring myself to. I trust you can find the owner?"

"I can."

"And for the other items?" Mrs. Rowley asked and Wilhelmina nodded.

She opened a drawer and removed a small, locked box and set it on the table. She handed Wilhelmina a key. Inside the box, everything that had been stolen since Mr. Swinton's death appeared to be there. She pushed through the objects. Some pieces of silver, some rings, a string of pearls. All items easily misplaced.

Mrs. Rowley looked down. "I hope you don't think too poorly of me."

She didn't. Mrs. Rowley had been desperate to get away.

"Can you... I don't want to go to prison for this. But I don't know..."

Wilhelmina reached out to her and took her hand. "Don't worry. She would understand." Thea was upset that the comb was missing, but with the way she behaved about Molly's secret marriage and the way she behaved about Wilhelmina's own marriage, she thought that Thea wouldn't begrudge Mrs. Rowley taking any attempt to escape."And I can return the other items."

"Thank you." Mrs. Rowley looked away. "Those servants didn't deserve to take the blame."

Wilhelmina took a breath. "Did you also take a bracelet the night Mr. Swinton... the night Simon died?"

Mrs. Rowley frowned, her brow furrowing up in concentration. "I don't remember one. If I took one, I must have sold it." She shook her head. "I'm sorry. I really thought I needed to."

Wilhelmina squeezed Mrs. Rowley's hand again. She wouldn't say that it was all right, because it wasn't. But Wilhelmina didn't plan to out the lady before her as a thief to all of society. She had been desperate and deserved a chance to make right what she could. She wouldn't get that in prison and it wasn't only her life that would be ruined if she was arrested. It was better this way.

***

"How did the meeting go?" James asked as he pulled out a chair for her. Wilhelmina sat down with a sigh.

"It went well."

His brow raised. "It doesn't seem like it went well."

"It did." She clenched her hands. "It just brought up some unpleasant memories."

He nodded.

"Where's Thea? I thought she was meeting us."

James smirked. "A message came that she's running late." He fought back laughter. "She was with the Inspector."

Inspector Thayne was becoming a familiar sight at Prescott House. He came by most evenings after work and often joined them for dinner when they dined at home, much to Lady Astermore's delight.

Wilhelmina held the comb out to James.

"This was the comb that went missing?" he asked as he took it and held it up to examine it with a critical eye. "An interesting gift. No wonder she was so upset to lose it."

"I couldn't get your aunt's bracelet back. I'm sorry."

James shook his head. "Emma is free because of you. That's what truly matters." His brow furrowed and he ran his fingers across the teeth of the comb. "What bracelet?"

"She said it was her grandmother's."

"I saw Emma wearing her grandmother's bracelet last night." James chuckled. "I guess she had it in her room all along."

Wilhelmina laughed.

CHARACTERS

James Poyntz - a journalist at his uncle's newspaper.

- birth parents: Vivien Prescott-Pryce and Stephen Bantry.
- adopted by: Arthur and Lucy Poyntz - deceased.
- ward of: Neville and Helen Poyntz - Nevile and Arthur were brothers.

Wilhelmina Allen (previously Wilhelmina Livingston) - After her husband's death, Wilhelmina decided to revert to her maiden name and become a private investigator.

Scotland Yard & Private Investigators

Detective Inspector Thomas Haddington
Detective Inspector Leslie Thayne
Gabriel Shaw - a private investigator who helps Wilhelmina out.

Poyntz

Emma Poyntz - James' cousin and Lady Charlie's friend.
Helen Poyntz - James' aunt and Emma's mother.
Neville Poyntz - James' uncle and Emma's father, owner of *The West End Gazette.*
Muse - James' beagle.

Astermore

Lady Theodora "Thea" Prescott-Pryce - James' half-sister.
Vivien Prescott-Pryce - The Dowager Countess of Astermore - Thea, Cecil, and James' mother. She was married to Matthew Prescott-Pryce before his death. Often called "The Countess" by the residents of Prescott House to keep from confusing her with her mother-in-law, Prudentia Prescott-Pryce.
Matthew Prescott-Pryce - the late Earl of Astermore - deceased - Thea and Cecil's father, Vivien's husband, Diana's brother.
Cecil Prescott-Pryce - Earl of Astermore - Thea's brother and James' half-brother.
Ilene Prescott-Pryce - Countess of Astermore - Cecil's wife and formally Thea's school friend.

Colonel Stephen Bantry - James' biological father.

Ravenholm

Malcolm McNeil - Earl of Ravenholm - Thea and Cecil's uncle.
Diana McNeil - Countess of Ravenholm - Matthew Prescott-Pryce's sister, Thea and Cecil's aunt, friend of Helen Poyntz.
Anthony McNeil - Lord Auldkirk - heir to Ravenholm - Thea and Cecil's cousin.
Lady Charlotte "Charlie" McNeil - Anthony's younger sister and Emma Poyntz's friend - Thea and Cecil's cousin.

LADY THEA'S WORLD

Lady Theodora has her own series of adventures in her historical cozy mystery series set 1910, about six months prior to the story in *Murder at the Midnight Ball.*

Murder on the Flying Scotsman

As the 1910 London Season comes to an end, it's time for Lady Theodora Prescott-Pryce's annual pilgrimage to visit her cousins in Scotland. Accompanied by only her maid, Molly, she thinks she's in for another long, dull trip aboard the Flying Scotsman.

The last thing she expects to find as they departed from London is a body in her compartment. Despite Molly being accused of the murder, Thea knows her maid is innocent.

Aided by a young Scotland Yard inspector and an American heiress, Thea uses the detective skills she learned from reading Sherlock Holmes to track down the real murderer, but will she find them before they can strike again?

ACKNOWLEDGMENTS

Cover art designed by Jessica Baker.

Art design by dmytrobosnak, sketchify, twemoji, lesiahnatiuk, and gengdev on Canva.com.

ABOUT THE AUTHOR

Named for the famous fictional mystery writer Jessica Fletcher, Jessica Baker picked up a pen when she was in elementary school and never set it down.

Jessica lives in sunny Central Florida and is a member of the National Sisters in Crime. When she's not writing, she works at a university and freelances as a camera assistant in film which provides plenty of inspiration for her stories.

To learn more about Jessica and her books, visit her at www.jessicabakerauthor.com and for the latest information, subscribe to her newsletters.